Mountains of Antrana

Book Three of the Erskan Trilogy

First Edition

Published by The Nazca Plains Corporation
Las Vegas, Nevada
2008

ISBN: 978-1-934625-02-6

Published by

The Nazca Plains Corporation ®
4640 Paradise Rd, Suite 141
Las Vegas NV 89109-8000

PUBLISHER'S NOTE
Mountains of Antrana is a work of fiction created wholly by *K. McVey's* imagination. All characters are fictional and any resemblance to any persons living or deceased is purely by accident. No portion of this book reflects any real person or events.

Editor, Karen Martin
Cover Art and Illustration, Michael Manning (www.thespidergarden.net)
Art Director, Blake Stephens

Acknowledgements

For Miss Chrysty:
  a. Sadistic
  b. Creative
  c. Leather
  d. All of the Above!

Mountains of Antrana

Book Three of the Erskan Trilogy

First Edition

K. McVey

Contents

Introduction

There was a time when I, Sheri Jordan, thought that a slave was someone who possessed no power, no ambition, nor personality.

That was before I worked on Taleon.

After graduating, I took my degree in Criminal Justice, caught the wave known as the "Expansion," and left Earth.

I came across a job posting for a security officer and arranged off-world travel. But I missed the connection and spent the night in an orbiting transit station in the Robbins System. There I met a man returning from his vacation. Lieutenant Reginald Burgess, Robbins Station Security Officer. Hell, he looked old even back then!

I canceled my flight and worked for Burgess almost six years when he finally convinced me to pack up everything again and move farther out, to Taleon of all places. Taleon is on the edge of nowhere.

It was a pay raise, a promotion, and I didn't have to work nights all the time.

I made a name for myself putting away bad guys. It was mostly minor stuff. Until Louis Corrigan came to town.

Corrigan was a Class A bad motherfucker. He was a gun runner, murderer, extortionist, escapee, and so on.

One dull afternoon I found inconsistencies in the station logistics records. I put together a team and we caught Corrigan by complete surprise. We held him six days until the closest Federal Ranger, Alexi Malind arrived to take him away.

Tall, dark-haired, and strong, Alexi made an entrance one would not expect: he was friendly, warm, and pretty damn funny.

Alexi and Captain Burgess were long-time friends. After reliving old war stories, Alexi hung out with my crew. We discovered we shared a love for ice hockey and we had the same dark sense of humor.

I went to his overnight quarters to fuck him. But I had just got his clothes off when all hell broke loose.

Corrigan had set up a diversion and escaped from the holding cell. He took out a couple of our officers on his way to a space craft.

Alexi, in true Ranger form, gave chase.

Captain Burgess got one of our extra-planetary crafts up an hour later and we pursued the cold interstellar trail.

We looked for hours.

We looked for days.

Alone, I searched for months.

Until…

And only then did I understand what it means to be a slave: to possess selfless power, unfailing determination, and strength of character.

I learned this before my time in the lands of Asil.

But what I did not know, at first, was that I set off a series of events that forever changed a world and forever changed my life.

This is what happened…

Chapter One
Cordiality

The first series of beeps only made me roll over.

The second series of beeps caused me to inch closer to the side of the seat until my hip pressed against the faux leather armrest.

It was the third series of beeps that made my eyes pop open.

The lower right control panel highlighted a sector of space by drawing a blue-green three-dimensional sphere.

There was a single red dot in the center of the celestial representation. The dot flashed twice on the screen.

The incessant indicator beeps chimed. I reached over to the panel and tapped the "mute" button.

Almost a year later.

Search teams, by the dozens, had arrived.

Grid patterns were established.

Teams fanned out.

After a month the number of search teams was cut in half.

After the second month there remained only two teams.

By the third month there was no official effort.

I convinced the Alberon Mining Corporation to loan a twenty year-old light ore hauler to me as a favor. It was slow in real-space and only moderately decent while in Corona space; I used it every third weekend.

After the logical trajectories were exhausted, search teams switched to the best-guess mode.

Those had been exploited.

And since I was the only mother fucker that cared enough to keep looking for Roberts and Alexi, I now searched on wild-ass-guess mode.

Besides, there wasn't anything else to do on the weekends at Taleon base.

Everything on this ore hauler was manual; I stabbed the "record" button.

"Sheri Jordan's report on twenty-eight July, '42," I said aloud. "Was in a coasting pattern in Sector Eight, King, Mary, Three-Five, when scanners detected an anomaly. Will take a quick glance. Too fuckin' far to transmit back to the Ranger station at Vega Melbourne. Will investigate and, if there is anything worth looking at, jump back to the closest transmitter relay and send an update."

I altered course and aimed the scarred and dented ore hauler toward the unidentified star system.

The planetary bodies were drawn on the screen as the scanners collected the data.

I twisted the cap off a plastic bottle of Mitey-Boostr, the latest caffeine-amplified fruit-flavored, protein, carbohydrate, sucrose, and fiber substitute – also known as "space" food. My lips tingled before the liquid even foamed down my throat. This stuff had to be bad for you. I put the bottle between my thighs.

The reason for the anomaly was still not clear. I had chased down thirteen such dead-ends over the last eight months.

"Now that's fuckin' interesting," I said aloud.

There were several planets, spread-out in an elliptical orbit around the star. It was not too unlike Sol...home.

One planet, third from the star, had a ring of moons around it, and the scanners detected a single electrical pulse from one of the orbiting rocks.

It took thirty minutes until I was within a few miles of the moon, one of the smaller ones.

The planet below was covered with clouds; however I could see large land masses and a hell of a lot of water.

"Real fuckin' interesting. Look at all that water. Fuck!"

And clouds.

It could be habitable.

I looked at the screen to read additional incoming data.

There was a trace dose of radiation coming off a couple of the larger moons, which were about a quarter of the planet's circumference away from my location. The scanners were unable to identify the radiation type. I adjusted the sensors without success.

The sensors did, however, pinpoint a pulse signal on the nearby moon.

I moved within fifty feet of a three-foot by six-inch metal object in orbit.

"Okay, so having a ore hauler is finally going to come in handy," I said.

It took a few minutes' work, but I managed to open a side loading bay and take a swipe with a robot to seize the object.

I secured the bay and moved the craft several miles distant from the moon before setting a geosynchronous orbit around the planet.

After another sip of the toxic drink, I placed the bottle in my customized cup holder and unbuckled the safety straps.

What that meant, really, was that I pressed the duct tape against the bottle to hold it against the instrument panel.

It was a short walk to the rear hatch.

The air recycled into the cargo deck.

Again, slowly.

Agh. Real slow. This ship did not win any speed records, inside or outside.

The green light flashed on the first of two doors. I opened both and walked onto the deck, holding the ceiling with my finger-tips and being careful to keep my magnetic boots solidly on the deck.

The object was charred and cracked along all surfaces.

I rolled it over with a tap of my right boot. There was no indication of what it was; but it did have a miniscule power cell. It *looked* old.

I removed the one-inch long, slim power cell from the mounting bracket.

It also looked old. There was a series of numbers on it, but nothing that made sense or placed the date.

I grabbed both pieces and walked back to the cockpit.

Just to be sure, I pointed the nose of the ore hauler to the planet and performed another sensor sweep.

Nothing.

Another dead end.

Dead end number fourteen.

About time to head to the next wild-ass-guess area, anyhow, and then home to Taleon. Alberon needed their ship in a few days.

I decided to take a loop around the planet to collect data. Hell, they might even name it after me.

Planet Jordan.

Planet Sheri.

No.

Sheria. Sher re ah. Nicely sounding name for a new planet.

I turned left, away from the larger moons, and started an escape trajectory to the dark side of Sheria.

If I got home in the next two days I could watch last week's hockey game when the data feed arrived.

Another sip of drink.

The weird taste on my tongue was likely that of melting tooth enamel.

"Gova. Treva."

It was a female voice, broadcast over the cockpit speakers.

I spit the liquid out of my mouth and onto my flight suit.

The computer display lit up with new data, and a bright red flashing letter that identified a federal police frequency.

Then the data on the screen went blank - - no signal.

"What the fuck?"

I slowed the ore hauler to a stop.

I fired the maneuvering thrusters and rotated one-hundred eighty degrees. Then I retraced the flight path.

Yes, the high-rate scan was active. The system was looking at all civilian, police, military, and federal frequencies.

My display flashed again and displayed the frequency ID.

"Fo. Dee Nat. Treva."

It was a female voice.

I put the hauler into a stationary position.

"Where is that?" I asked as I fingered a few switches.

There!

A region, only a few hundred square miles, was over the planet where the unusual radiation was dampened.

The larger moons, on the other side of the planet, cast an expansive interference field.

But this spot was clear.

I pressed the transmit button.

"Identify yourself," I ordered.

There was no reply.

"Identify yourself. Now."

I waited another ten seconds.

New data streamed in to the sensors and scrolled on my instrumentation display.

It was from an automatic distress beacon.

My eyes fixated on the identifier: C-308, A. Malind, 2837-NE0-2878.

"Arfla? Yet beer Yannta. Bay? Gova."

It wasn't static on the radio; the female voice spoke in a language other than English. It wasn't Japanese or Dutch either.

"Identify yourself immediately," I said again.

"Who will be speaking?" I heard a different woman's voice.

"Jordan, Sheri. Taleon Base Security Chief. Who is this?"

"You is a Earth trenama hunter?"

"A what? Who is this?" I demanded, my patience growing thin. "Is this a joke?"

"Jordan Sheri Taleon, you is crime hunter?"

Crime hunter?

"Yes. This is the last time I ask you. Who is this? What are you doing on this frequency?"

"Jordan Sheri Taleon, you are to find and look at Alecksee?"

Alexi!

"Yes! Alexi. You know him? Is he here?"

There was a pause.

"Is he here?"

"I think Earth speak is, I am sorry, do not know all words. Alexi would tell you in the Earth speak is to say 'sort of.'"

Sort of?

What the fuck?

Earth speak?

"Where are you?" I finally demanded. I looked at a sensor display. "Never mind, I see you. I am coming and you better have answers for me."

I heard several exclamations and brisk talk in their language.

"Jordan Sheri Taleon. I will make a favor at you. You have a Tamagra, maybe? It will make bad times for my people to look at Tamagra. You have meet me at other… other ground place?"

"Yes. You go find a ground place and I will meet you. Just leave your radio on."

"Leave the radio, sorry?" she asked.

"Take it with you, but do not turn it to 'off,'" I explained.

"Thank you."

"And you are?" I asked, yet again.

"Meet me on the ground place at a twenty-five Earth minutes. My name called is Torino Tural."

After a moment I had a fix on the radio transmitter. The communications system pegged it as "C-308/2838.1003.skh." No question that it was an Earth Alliance Ranger frequency that was attached to Alexi's Tamagra.

The ore hauler broke through the clouds at approximately fifteen thousand feet.

I banked a few degrees on the descent to get a better view below.

There was an expansive body of water on my left; a forest and coastal area south and east, plains northeast, and a city slightly to my right-middle.

Much farther ahead, partially obscured by clouds and distance, was an impressive mountain range.

The navigation system diagrammed the terrain below and superimposed a green dot indicating the Ranger radio. It was moving south at a surprising rate of speed.

Three other green dots appeared in the immediate area. Several radios were in use.

The particular radio of my interest moved south of my position.

I turned around to follow.

Finally Alexi's radio stopped moving.

I held fast and hovered at ten-thousand feet until twenty-five minutes passed. At this altitude it was too difficult to identify any specific ground movement.

What the fuck does "sort of" mean, anyhow?

I put the ore hauler into a fifteen degree descent and spiraled downward in a quarter-mile wide helix. This ship was slow. Though it was made only for short-range loads, it was still pretty big.

At five-thousand feet I could see a path through the forest and a small clearing. There were multiple people on the ground.

At two-thousand feet I could observe six figures on horseback.

And I would need a much larger area to land.

I stopped and adjusted the navigational display.

Looking southeast I saw a wide clearing. It was approximately six-hundred feet by one-thousand feet, roughly rectangular. It was still too small, but would have to do. It was a quarter-mile away. I turned and moved, hoping they would figure out the problem with landing at the location they selected.

It took a minute or so until I reached the location and made a vertical descent.

The ore hauler rocked and creaked as it crushed anywhere between ten and twenty of the big trees that were unfortunate enough to be under the eleven-thousand ton craft.

Entire tree trunks shattered. Sixty-foot high chunks of wood ejected from the side of the ship.

Nice landing.

I took another sip of the drink and taped it to the instrument panel.

Unsnap the seatbelts.

Gun.

I grabbed the StacGun.

No, need a bigger gun.

I returned the handgun to the box and grabbed onto a Browning.

Then I stepped toward the hatch.

No. Get the smaller gun also.

So I unlocked the StacGun again and holstered it.

A tap of the hatch with my fingertip; the door slid open.

Oh, fuck. Is the air safe to breathe?

Too late now.

I sucked in.

In fact, the air was pretty nice. Fresh. Much better than the imported air on Taleon. Far much better than the goddamned recycled air inside the ore hauler.

The temperature was mild outside. Partly cloudy. Mid-day?

I stepped down the short ladder onto the grass.

My boots sank as the wide blades reached my knees.

Again, I felt like slapping myself. What if the grass was poisonous or there were flesh-eating bugs?

To my left and behind me was the cargo body of the ore hauler. The surface, despite being coated in FrictionLite, still pushed out waves of heat that obscured the view of the dead trees.

Okay, maybe I had crushed more than twenty trees. Looked like. . . forty?

Plenty of trees around here, though. Didn't seem like they would miss having these.

I heard women's voices to the right.

After a moment they broke through the trees and stopped.

We were only twenty feet apart. My mouth opened and hung there.

Five women. They were on horses Um, no. Not really horses. Camels with horse-like legs. There was a riderless horse pulled by one of the women.

One woman was in front of the others. She crossed her arms before her and looked down and across at me. She was stunning. Black, spiky hair that blew in the breeze, rounded eyes, a row of gold earrings, black – almost purple – leather top trying to hold down ample breasts, long gloves, matching short leather skirt, and wicked-looking front-laced calf-high boots.

The handle of a sword appeared from behind her back and over her shoulder.

But what really caught my attention was the StacGun that was holstered on her right thigh.

The other four women were similarly dressed. One had the Federal radio holstered to her belt.

All of them were armed with swords.

"Jordan Sheri Taleon," the woman said. "I am Tural."

"Tural. I am Jordan."

Tural cocked her head slightly. "Browning. You not needing that. You can but bring with you. Is okay."

I relaxed my grip on the larger automatic weapon.

"Jordan, you will please much understand my English speak. I am not speaking as well."

"I can understand you," I nodded. "You know Alexi?"

"Yes."

"How do you know Alexi? Where is he?"

"He is my frey."

"What is a 'frey'?" I asked.

"Alexi is frey. I am owner."

"What? Where is he?"

A woman on Tural's right side, my left, moved closer and spoke in their language.

"We must know before we talk to you," Tural said. "It is a worry we have that you is not a friend of my Alexi. How is you know Alexi?"

"I will answer that question," I told the woman. "Then you answer my questions."

She nodded.

"Alexi is a police Ranger. He came to my base... my planet, like this, well not like this. But he left chasing a criminal almost a year ago."

"The trenama," Tural nodded again. "Louis Corrigan."

My eyes widened. "Yes."

"Corrigan is a trenama. . . a bad man on here our world. Corrigan and a nearby female made together a. . . a leading of people and the people suffers for them. Then they make war onto my people. We are Erskan. Corrigan use Earth firearms. Alexi help us make win of war and save Erskan women and frey. We go to Corrigan and make war. This is here, ground place of Treaslok. Now it is Erskan land and I am owner of it.

"From seas of Antrana of Erskan main city, Alexi make us help to bring ships of war to Treaslok. On the fight in seas, Alexi in ships of war crash. Corrigan take away Alexi."

Tural's countenance wavered for a moment. She closed her eyes. "Corrigan take my Alexi and Cinzia's Mermak."

The woman on Tural's right recognized the last word and looked at me.

I could read a sense of loss in her eyes also.

"Tural," I asked. "Is Alexi alive?"

"Is Alexi live?" she repeated.

I nodded.

"We have thinks that yes, is live."

"Where is Roberts?" I asked her.

"Roberts?" Tural asked. "Is other Earth man?"

"Yes."

She shook her head. Apparently that was also their way of showing "no."

"Tamagra on fire and goes into sand," Tura said. "No Roberts a live."

"What kind of ships does Corrigan have?" I asked. "Does he have a . . . one of these?" I pointed at the craft behind me.

The Cinzia woman shook her head "no."

"She is know to learn English," Tural said.

"When did this happen?" I asked.

"Alexi and Mermak taken by Corrigan three days ago," Cinzia said.

"Do you know where?"

"Yes. We make good think," Cinzia replied after contemplating a reply.

I crossed my arms before me also. If the people holding Alexi were also three or four centuries behind Tural and her group this would be no problem. "Then you just need to point where to me and I'll go get him."

Tural smiled for the first time.

"You will be our welcome of guest? We show you on mapping paper what we know is where Alexi and Mermak and you can help then for us?"

"Gladly," I nodded.

"Do you can ride?" Tural asked. A woman pulled the rope of a horse camel forward.

"Uh. No."

"You will learn how can ride now," Tural smiled again.

Two of the women rode toward the craft and dismounted.

"They will keep safe of it," Tural told me.

"No one could harm it," I told her. The hatch was shut and locked.

Cinzia looked at the expanse of flattened trees and laughed in a funny sound that was like "oy, oy, oy."

Cinzia handed the ropes, or lines, or whatever they are called, to me. She clapped my left shoulder with her palm and pointed at herself, "Cinzia."

"Jordan," I told her.

She put her hand up and wiggled her finger in a "follow-me" motion.

"This is quite a welcome," I told Tural. "I bet Alexi was really impressed when he met your people."

Tural and Cinzia looked at me. Then they looked at one another. "Oy, oy, oy," Tural laughed, turned her horse camel around, and rode on.

* * * * *

After a mile of riding we were met on the gravel path by ten additional warriors, all female.

All female.

All no-nonsense.

All armed with swords and an occasional bow.

The ten women followed. However, ahead I saw two other warriors, moving at our pace, keeping an even distance from us. They were apparently an escort.

We reached a few houses. They looked very old Europe-style. At least, from the picture videos I had seen.

Four more women warriors appeared on the side of the road, remaining still as we rode past them. They saluted Tural or Cinzia, both riding ahead of me.

Tural and Cinzia were talking to one another until Tural nodded. She raised her right hand. I practically ran my camel horse into the back of her camel horse.

"Sorry," I said. "I didn't know what you meant by that, at first, raising your hand."

"It is no worries," Tural smiled. "I am of so honor to have Earth female here."

Cinzia turned in her saddle and opened her hands in front of her, in an encouraging gesture to me.

"Jordan," Tural said, her smile fading. "I have in prior tell to you about Erskan life. It is not like the Earth living."

"Yes?" I said. I looked around at the rural surroundings. "I can see."

Quite primitive. They did not need to apologize to me.

Tural shook her head.

Cinzia rubbed her chin. Then, "Here is good for you."

Tural nodded. "In Earth living, you have female and male together, yes you do?" She held her two hands in the air, palms up, hands level with one another.

"Yes, usually."

Sometimes.

"In Erskan living, it is not." She lowered her right hand to her thigh and raised her left hand a few inches.

She emphasized her left hand and said, "Female."

She emphasized her right hand, "Male."

"Uh. So you have a female in charge of your city?" I already guessed that Tural was a leader of sorts here.

"No, Jordan." She shook her head. "Not in only city. In all livings."

"What do you mean by all living?"

"All things. Everything."

Maybe our English was not translating.

"Alexi uses Earth word," Tural said. "I tell you his word. All males are 'slaves.'"

"Did you say 'slaves?'"

"Yes. In our world we have a one male for each of many females. Males are made safe and owned."

"Wait a second," I told her. "What is *your* word for 'slave?'"

Tural paused, for a second or two. Then she spoke again, "Erskan word for 'slave' is 'frey.'"

I sat back in the saddle.

"You said, earlier, that Alexi was your frey. He is your slave?"

Tural nodded. "He wears the Tural collar." Then she looked directly into my eyes. "Alexi is my slave."

I shook my head. "I don't believe that. Alexi would never be anyone's slave."

Cinzia nodded.

That was fucking ridiculous!

Did they drug him?

What did they do to Alexi?

"And you let him be captured by Corrigan?" I asked.

Tural's face faded into a frown.

I obviously touched a sensitive point.

She turned her camel around.

"Wait, please," I said. "I. I did not want to sound like that."

Tural glanced once over her shoulder and then continued riding.

Cinzia's eyes drilled into mine. She pointed at Tural's. "Torino Tural loves on the Alexi." Then she rode after Tural.

I tried to make the camel catch up to them, but they were intentionally keeping a distance.

Smooth fucking move: I just pissed-off one of the leaders.

Hopefully she won't tell the queen.

Tural loves on the Alexi?

Tural loves Alexi?

Tural loves him.

Alexi a slave?

Not a chance in hell.

Within a minute we reached the outskirts of the city.

High trees gave way to a few buildings.

There were a few women outside. The civilians were not dressed in the manner of the sixteen women riding with our pack.

They looked like an industrial people; everyone worked on the outside of their house or building or garden. Each building had several flower boxes with brightly-colored flowers overflowing the edge. The gravel road changed to well-swept cobblestone.

I noted metal grilles at intervals on the side of the road: they had sewage.

Each building also sported a narrow flag, two bright blue stripes, one white, and one red, hung on a pole jutting out from the wall.

I made a mental snapshot of the first turn we made. I did not want to get lost if Alexi and I were making a all-out sprint for the ore hauler.

A wooden wagon was parked at one intersection. Three warrior women stood about, handing fabric bags to the first male I had seen.

He was short. Approximately twenty years of age. He wore a long, gray, ankle-length skirt!

Calf-high boots were visible on the side slit of his skirt. He wore no shirt. But he did have a black metal band around his neck.

A collar?

A *slave* collar?

Why didn't he try to run away?

Because those swords look sharp, moron!

Two of the women warriors at the wagon were dressed similarly to the Erskans here. Well, not exactly. Now I noticed that one woman of our group wore a different style of uniform. It was gray, not purplish, less shiny and loosely cut, and – well, it looked worn and of lesser quality. She also had no metal insignia on her outfit; whereas the Erskans had different kinds of metal circles and bars affixed to wrist bands and bands around their biceps.

The city became dense. One-story buildings gave way to four-story buildings with shops on the bottom floor and residential units above.

Next escape point: I burned a street sign into my memory. The characters on the sign were completely foreign. They were made of graceful, flowing symbols, similar in style to Katakana.

By now we had passed by a thousand people. Or, actually, a thousand women and probably a hundred men. All of the men had black bands around the neck.

Collars.

We reached the first of several military checkpoints. It was manned – uh, operated – by six Erskan women and one of the other warriors. All of them came to attention and waved our party through the wood gate. Several nearby women constructed a metal mesh, chain-link style of fencing. The immediate area looked damaged. Chunks of nearby buildings were missing. I had failed to notice when cobblestone roads changed to intricately placed multi-color brick.

We picked up another two warriors as escort.

Shortly the road widened. It was clogged with women and men. Children, of both sexes, were also outside, playing. Everyone, without exception, stopped to look at our party as we rode by.

I could imagine what Alexi thought when he rode into the city. No doubt they were impressed with him. He probably got a fucking parade. Earth man coming to save the day and all that. It would be just like the Ranger ego.

Or maybe it was another city?

Too much information to absorb.

We turned slightly to the right.

Escape point: snapshot of a store that sold candles. I bet a place like this goes through a big stack o' candles every night.

To my left side was a sea port.

Really, it was the remains of a sea port.

Dozens of ships listed to one side or the other. Everything had been burned. A charcoal odor permeated the air.

Blackened hulks of ships were scattered about like toys on the far end of the port, nearest the sea.

It wasn't that a simple fire went through the docks; it looked like it had been bombed.

Tural raised her hand.

This time I managed to stop without bumping into her camel horse.

"You see?" she pointed to the sea port.

"Yes. You did this?" I asked.

"Erskan did this," she said. "Alexi idea to make it do."

"Alexi's plan?" I confirmed.

Tural nodded.

A large gathering of women in civilian clothes performed clean-up on the closest edge of the sea port. A couple of men – slaves – shuttled buckets among the women.

Two ships were anchored at the end of the sea port. They were clearly untouched by the battle and, I assumed, were Erskan.

I laughed.

"Yannow," I told Tural. "That doesn't surprise me."

"Sorry?" she asked.

"I believe you – about Alexi having this idea." He would probably like the drama of a big battle.

"You know my frey for a longer time?" Tural asked.

Was she concerned that I was involved with him?

"No. Only two days. We worked together."

"You want him as your frey?" she asked.

Now we got to Tural's real concern.

"No! I do not want a slave. I am here to help him." Just to make sure she understood me I repeated, "No, I do not want a slave. Any slave."

Tural nodded. I saw a bit of relief on her expression. She turned and continued riding.

The woman called Cinzia took her radio and spoke in their language for a few sentences.

Then we turned another corner and I had a direct line-of-sight to a castle, a considerable distance away.

I almost forgot to take another escape check.

The street was quite wide. Lamp posts lined the street in front of many businesses. Camels – oh, hell, horses – moved to the side as our armed escort ensured there was no delay.

All activity ceased as we rode among thousands of people.

The Erskan warriors in the front of our group looked straight ahead; however Tural and Cinzia swept the sides of the street with their eyes and, on occasion, tipped their chin in an acknowledgement of a friendly wave.

"Seems like a busy place!" I said loudly.

Tural did not look back, but nodded her head.

We came to a wall that was partially destroyed. Teams of women were busy constructing more metal fencing. Only this was different wire: barbed wire.

"Alexi?" I asked.

Cinzia turned her head and nodded.

It occurred to me that, as a kid, I loved to watch the really-old classic movies. There had been a show about the "Main Directive," or the "Prevention Directive." Basically it had a premise that advanced civilizations were not supposed to interfere with primitive cultures.

There was a new gate under construction.

We passed under the new stone blocks and I looked up to see two Erskan warriors protecting a tripod-mounted Crest-Leeland machine gun.

Cinzia did not wait for my question. She simply nodded.

No fucking "Main Directive" here now.

There was a second wall and gate. It was practically demolished. Nobody did any reconstruction work here.

And then we stopped at the foot of the castle.

It was a big castle.

A real honest-to-goddamned castle.

Ten stories high. Or more. It had spires. Small windows dotted the sides at evenly spaced intervals. Women looked down at us, bow in hand.

"Seha?" I heard a man's voice below.

Surprised, I pulled my eyes away from gazing upward.

A man stood beside my horse, below on my right. He wore a black, ankle-length leather skirt, black leather bands on his biceps, and a silver metal collar. The collar appeared to be made of polished steel. He was shirtless and tanned, or of a natural dark brown skin tone. And he was diminutive. In fact, all of the Erskans, and the other ones, were smaller in stature than Earth people.

I was fairly short among humans, Earth humans. But here I was the same height as their tallest people.

The man reached for my horse lines.

I handed them to him.

Beside Tural, another man got on his knees, to the gravel. Tural dismounted and stood onto the man's back as a stepping-point to the ground. Then she planted both of her booted feet on the ground.

The man kissed the top of her right boot!

Then he kissed her left boot!

Cinzia was equally received. As were a couple of other women in our group.

The man near me got onto his hands and knees.

Tural and Cinzia turned to look at me.

I wasn't sure what to do.

Then there were ten women waiting for me.

Goddammit!

Everyone looked at me.

Tural nodded to a fierce-looking warrior, "Visada, too dema de arralt eksa Jordan."

The warrior, armed with a large sword across her back, a knife on each thigh, and metal-spiked black leather gloves, moved over to my horse and offered her hand to me.

I took her right gloved hand in mine and slowly pulled my left leg over the horse. Then I put my right boot heel into the man's lower back. Visada reached over to my ankle and pulled my boot over to the middle of the man's backside, within the gap of my heel at his spine. She nodded.

I brought my other boot down and placed it next to my right.

She did not adjust it, so I must have got it right.

Then she pointed to the ground.

With her hand in mine, I gingerly stepped off the man's back and to the ground with both feet.

She continued to hold my hand, even though I pulled slightly, ready to distance myself from this.

She would not let me go.

The man turned his body. He pressed his face down to my right boot!

I wasn't so sure that Alexi got this level of treatment, come to think of it.

The man kissed my left boot.

The woman said something to him. He stood and grabbed the horse line and walked away with it.

The woman released my hand and smiled.

I didn't think this would ever happen to me.

I did my best to return a smile.

"Please, Jordan, pardon my mess," Tural said, as though she was quoting someone. We followed her into a set of heavy wood doors and into the castle.

After climbing a wide set of circular stairs I found myself in an expansive room that overlooked an even larger arched area one floor below.

Oil lamps brightened every inch of the castle.

We reached an area that was a hive of activity. Thirty, no forty or more female warriors moved about, all talking in their language. Most were Erskan, though there were a few of the Treasalokins present. There were perhaps five men, all slaves, walking about carrying food or drink or other supplies.

We came to a large table that sported multiple maps.

Most of the maps were made of a cloth material with black bold markings. But there were two maps made of crinkled paper.

I ran my fingertips on one of the two maps.

The room became deathly quiet as the others recognized there was someone else here that wasn't dressed like the others.

"Paper," I said in English.

Cinzia nodded. "Alexi."

I shook my head.

Is there anything he hasn't changed here?

Tural addressed the room and spoke rapidly in her language.

Women's eyes became wider and they fixated on me.

I felt very under-dressed for the occasion.

Especially in comparison to their spiffy, neat, polished, and attractively-tight leather uniforms.

My light-gray, one-piece flight suit was drab, loose-fitting, and completely unappetizing.

I didn't really plan to meet up with a whole goddamned planet of Amazon chicks today.

"Hello," I said.

Tural said something. There was a ripple of laughter and a few smiles.

Self-consciously I pulled on both sides of my jumpsuit to smooth the wrinkles.

Having worn this for two days, my clothes were not only funny looking, they were wrinkled.

Cinzia uttered what sounded like a command.

Most of the women returned to their work and the din of conversation increased again.

Still, several of the women stole a look in my direction from time to time.

Tural talked to a young woman. The young woman ran out of the room, apparently on an errand.

"Do you would like a drink?" Tural asked me.

I noticed that a particular warrior hovered nearby to my left.

"What does she want?" I asked.

"She is my watcher," Tural said, not taking her eyes away from the map. "She does not like you having the Browning – or the StacGun."

"What StacGun?" I asked, playing dumb.

A different woman, on the other side of the large table, waved her hand to me. She had on a pair of Daytonic glasses. It was a clash of style; the dark-blue, sleek titanium frames wrapped around her head with po arized clearsteel lenses. And her black leather, Amazon fighting uniform.

But the important thing was that she could clearly visually detect anything metal that I had on my person. Especially a Mark VII StacGun.

So I had been caught in a lie.

I laughed.

I was already heavily outgunned here. And then there were the swords. And bows and arrows. And the Crest-Leeland. And the radios. I would not win a fight here.

"Would you like to have my guns?" I asked Tural.

"No, Jordan Sheri. I would like most to have the honest of talk from you."

I nodded. I slung the Browning from my shoulder. I placed it on the table. Then I slowly unholsted my StacGun and placed it beside the machine gun.

"I am sorry," I told her. "Please take these."

Tural smiled.

She reached for the Browning, held it upright, and then presented it back to me in proper form.

Which I hadn't done…properly, that is.

It was clear that Alexi had trained them or this as well.

What else did they know how to use? I should not underestimate them again.

I wasn't going to refuse the offer from the queen. Clearly Tural was in charge here.

I took the Browning from her hands.

"Is there having more ammunition?" she asked, handing the StacGun to me.

"Not much," I said.

"You have a big sky wagon," Tural said. "It is much big than the Tamagra."

"My sky wagon is made for carrying big rocks."

"Platinum rocks?" Tural asked.

I blinked. "I wish."

"We fill it much big with platinum; you give us much more ammunition?"

I blinked again. Fill it? They saw how big the ore hauler is. "Uh, first, where is Alexi?"

Tural pointed to the map.

Then the young woman appeared, a rough-looking hardbound book held against her chest. Tural took it and opened the cover.

The pages were made of paper. They were held into the spine with thread.

"This could may help you learn," Tural said.

"What is it?" I took the book into my hands.

"My frey calls it his 'dictionary.'"

Tural's voice was casual when she mentioned that Alexi was her slave. I managed to only partially conceal my frown.

The first sheet had four rows of penciled-in text.

"apple" was the first word in English. Beside it were three squiggly symbols.

"'Tloy'" Cinzia said from over my shoulder.

I didn't really plan to be here long enough to need this. Grab Alexi, leave planet. My plan was simple.

"Thank you." I closed the book and pointed to the map. "Where is Alexi?"

Chapter Two
Observations and Greintol

Tural pointed to one of the maps and asked a gray-uniformed woman a question. Their speech was different than the native language in that it was less flowing and more guttural.

"Corrigan made a runfor to the —" Tural pointed upward on the map from the city.

"North?" I asked.

"Yes. He made a runfor to the north. These are mountains. It is only one way on this ground place to make enter into the —" she stopped again, frustrated. She waved her hands around, indicating the room. "Shenada?"

"Castle?" I asked.

She frowned. "Odek, dictionary," she reached out.

I handed Alexi's book to her. She flipped through to the back.

"Odek, yes, castle. Or Palace."

"I can take you there in my—" I paused. "In my space wagon."

Tural and Cinzia grinned.

"Yes, we want hope good that you want to move in that way," Tural nodded.

"We can look first. See what is there. Then make plans to go back," I said. I moved a step to the door, but they held still. "Well?"

They had a brief conversation.

Tural glanced at me a couple of times.

It sounded like the gray-uniformed warrior disagreed with the plan.

"We wait five Earth time hours," Tural told me. "It will be no day time. I cannot allow space wagon to fly over women in day time. You have seeing eye glasses for fly at no day time light?"

I looked at my wrist watch. "Okay. Five hours is good."

A man, wearing a long two-paneled black leather skirt, sandals, and a silver metal collar stopped beside me. He kept his eyes to the middle of my body as he extended a silver platter with several crystal glasses of a red-tinted liquid.

I took a glass and watched him move to the next woman.

The drink was sweet. Perhaps a fruit juice, not unlike cherry. I drained the glass with a second try.

Instantly another male… a male *slave*, was there with a platter to collect my empty glass.

Saying "male slave" was redundant here, come to think of it.

"Tural, where is the woman's room?" I asked her. I really had to go.

Tural looked about her. "It is all the woman's room," she said, frowning. "*All* of the lands are the woman's."

I opened the dictionary and pointed to an Erskan word.

"Brinkle," she said to a young woman. Then Tural pointed to a hall.

The female aide, probably sixteen or seventeen years of age, moved over to me and offered her hand. "Seha?"

I took her hand and she led me to one of the doors and my first experience with an alien toilet.

* * * * *

"The women wearing gray are not Erskan people?" I asked.

"They are Treaslok," Tural replied. Her hands were flat on the table. She leaned down slightly while looking at a map.

"You fought the Treaslok," I stated.

"Yes."

"They are here – working with you," I observed.

"Treaslok and Erskans fight for long year time," Tural said, turning to face me and resting her right hip against the side of the table. "But wars are always of time here. We have many much more women than frey. Women fight for the owning of frey. This makes a – a happening – of wars. But the wars here on Treaslok were much bad because Louis Corrigan made slaves of all – he made women-frey and frey. Treaslok fighted wars they did not want to fight. We won fight and bring war to Treaslok. Now we have not big hate for Treaslok. We will make small Treaslok women in part of us and make more big Treaslok women in more time."

"Women do all of the fighting?"

"There are many women," Tural said. "Alexi and I have much talk with about this. He says in Earth speak that Erskan women are 'disposable' and the war fights keep woman count low."

Fuck!

"Now you have no wars," I said, in an attempt to sound positive.

Tural laughed in their peculiar way, "Oy, oy, oy."

She turned to her map. "We are here in this ground place." She pointed to the east. "This is Busai. This is Breti. This is Hundra. All want to kill Treaslok."

"But you are here now."

"Yes. This is the 'fix' we are finding on ourselves."

"Oh," I said.

"Corrigan has make a offer to Busai leader 'Busai win fight on Treaslok, and Corrigan give Alexi to Busai.'"

"Why? Why do the Busai want Alexi?"

"Alexi knows much and has big of thought to make new mechanicals. With Alexi, Busai they much become powerful .. powerful and much large number of women."

Cinzia had come to stand beside Tural.

I addressed both of them, my hand pointing to the east of the Treaslok lands. "Could you meet with the Busais? Maybe they will listen to you talk. We could offer them something else."

Or I could bring a whole fucking Space Guard contingent here and they'd take care of this in a day. Five hovertanks would beat these primitive, Renn-Faire people to --

Cinzia smirked.

Tural looked at her for a moment and then returned to her map.

Cinzia pointed at Tural, "Torino Tural meeted with Busai leader, Kale. Kale made trap. Tural stick blade into Kale. Kale not wanting to talk at now with cut hand."

The gray-uniformed Treaslok woman spoke to Cinzia.

They exchanged several rapid sentences.

Tural turned about and asked a question, apparently surprised.

The Treaslok replied, her voice flat. She nodded.

Several of the women around us turned their heads and looked at Tural.

Tural shrugged her shoulders. Then she waved her hands in the air and said a word I couldn't catch. "Etra" or "Netra" or something like that.

"What?" I asked.

Tural tapped her fingers on her hip and stared beyond the Treaslok. Then Tural returned to her map.

"What?" I asked again.

Cinzia moved closer to me. She glanced over her shoulder at Tural. "I tell you Torino Tural cut Busai leader?"

"Yes, I got that."

Cinzia's eyes flickered at Tural and then back at me. "We have know now that Torino Tural also kill Busai leader *wetana*."

"What's that?"

I handed the dictionary to Cinzia. She flipped through several pages and handed it back to me. Her finger rested on a word.

"Oh, great," I said. "She killed her sister?"

"Wetana," Cinzia replied.

"I can bring much help," I told them. "I should have called for help already."

"What happen if when you bring more Earth people here?" Tural snapped her head toward me. "Earth people have made them bad things here. We had make wars, but not big wars. Now we have many – many – " she grabbed the dictionary from my hand turned to a page, and slammed it down. The sound of the book echoed in the room. "Now we have thirty and thousands women die because you came to Aervanta. I do not want more Earth people. I do not want more women die."

The room fell silent as the occupants turned toward us.

Tural raised her left hand and said a few words aloud. Everyone went back to their own business.

"Four Earth hours," Cinzia said to me. "Are you like to have food now?"

"Yes, I would."

Tural was quite the bitchy one. Friendly one moment; jumping on everyone's ass the next.

"I not speak well, but try," she told me.

Tural was consumed with her maps and aides. She barely noticed my departure.

* * * * *

"She is an angry person," I said aloud, wanting to see what Cinzia had to say.

Cinzia paused. I could see her forming the reply in her head. Then, "You might would see Sklera, her wetana."

"Is Tural the leader? The one in charge?"

"Yes. The Secura Torino. She is leader in ground place here of Treaslok only. Only Treaslok. Not Antrana. Sklera is leader of all Erskans across the seas of Antrana. Torino Sklera Kretahla, the Primera Torino."

"What is Antrana?"

"Antrana is Erskan home city ground place."

"Who are you?"

"I am high jurina for Torino Tural."

I blinked. A new word every minute.

We walked into a wide room, a canteen, which held eight long benches and chairs. Several women, all in uniform, sat at the tables eating. It did smell good, actually, and I felt my stomach grumble. I followed Cinzia until she sat at an unoccupied table.

I made a mental note of our location and path back to the main doorway.

"Who is the tall warrior that is watching me in the large room? She is older than you and Tural."

Cinzia seemed surprised that I had been aware.

I felt that my observation had earned a little respect from Cinzia.

"She is Jurina Korina Yannta. She is high jurina for Tural's wetana. She will be leaving of us tonight. There is problems on home of Antrana. Other peoples on Erskan borders are make us worry about them. Many Erskan warriors are now in Treaslok ground. We will make move on ships of warriors to home of Antrana soon."

"How many warriors?"

"I do not know how to make count."

The dictionary was on the table – maybe I should carry it with me for the next day or two until Alexi and I left this place.

I held out my finger. "One." Then my both hands. "Ten." Then flashed my fingers ten times. "One-hundred. And ten more is one-thousand."

Cinzia looked at her hands. "One thousand by ten and ten."

"Twenty-thousand?" I asked.

She nodded.

"Okay. We get Alexi back tonight, and I will move your warriors for you. I can surely put four-thousand in my ship. It would just be five trips back and forth."

"How many days?" she asked.

"Days?" I shook my head. "No. Hours. Uh. Is an hour here the same as an Earth hour?"

"Alexi says it is almost same. Our word is not 'hour' but Alexi teach English and Dutch to me." She smiled. "I like sound of Japon words, but is not easy. English is happy good."

"Good. That makes this easy. I was on a planet where the minutes were – never mind. This would be five trips. We will spend more time loading and unloading your soldiers than flying across the sea. It doesn't look very wide. Three hours for the entire deal. Maybe Four."

Cinzia's eyes widened. She held up four fingers. "Sorry. Four hours?"

"It might get crowded. But shouldn't be too much of a problem. A thousand soldiers per deck, four decks. No chairs. But they would only be in flight for twenty minutes."

Cinzia managed a smile, flashing perfect white teeth to me. It was clear that she had a thought: "We could use the space wagon. To make warriors land in other ground places?"

Ah. These chicks were really thinking ahead, weren't they?

"Maybe."

"We could land four-thousand warriors at the behind of Busai warriors."

"Maybe."

"Or in mountain palace."

"Probably."

"Sorry?"

"Maybe," I said. "More than maybe. First thing, we get Alexi. Then we talk about other help."

Cinzia bit her lip. "It is my hope that my frey is can be found."

"Mermaid?" I asked.

"'Mermak,'" she corrected, her voice soft, almost a whisper.

"Does the name 'Cinzia' mean anything?" I asked, trying to change the subject – to take her away from thinking of her missing slave man.

"Yes. All Erskan names have a mean of around us."

"Try that again?"

"Erskan names have… a mean to the plants and animals and up in air."

"Nature."

"Natura, yes." She grinned at me, "My name is have mean to a plant of colors."

"I'm sure it is a pretty plant."

"You not like Alexi. Alexi never ask this question."

"Yannow, he is a guy – a man. They don't have a clue about that." I looked at her fingers. "He's never asked about your rings, has he?"

"Sorry?"

I pointed to her rings. "Rings. They are very pretty."

"No. Alexi not ask of rings. Our Erskan frey ask about meaning of clues and rings and names."

"Really?" I asked, surprised.

"Maybe it would be happy good if Earth men were frey, too."

I left that one alone. But I did nod once. I think.

A man approached. I expected him to cower when he asked a question, but rather he stood straight. He bowed and then looked at Cinzia.

"Greintol a ene vi de irik," she said to him.

He nodded, left our table, and stepped through a doorway.

"I will make guess you like same food as Alexi," she said. "Greintol is his most like food. Greintol is not having much times. Uh, special good for special time."

"Thank you."

I wondered what Alexi liked to eat. Hopefully it was not seafood. The Erskans had a number of ships and it wouldn't be too much of a stretch to find a big plate of fish here in a moment.

"We are happy good that you Jordan are here. A Earth woman is happy good for us."

"Tural did not sound happy about that," I pointed to the door which led to the war room.

"She is not happy about Corrigan. She has much to worry with on of her. To now make strong Erskans here over Treaslok. To row make fight on Busai. To now make fight to Corrigan. But you are here and this is happy good."

The collared man brought a tray with two ceramic bowls, two transparent glasses filled with water, I presumed, and spoons. He placed the tray onto the table slightly out of our reach. He pulled a single blue cloth from the tray and placed it on Cinzia's lap.

I leaned back slightly as he placed a blue cloth on my lap.

Then he sat the bowls before us each, always serving Cinzia first, and then the glass, spoon, and a napkin. Everything was in a perfect position and an even distance from each other items, and the edge of the table.

I could smell hot food, but could not figure out what it was.

"Greintol," Cinzia said with a thoughtful smile.

The Erskan "special food" was going to be boiled shrimp or other sea critter. I knew it. Maybe something with tentacles.

Do not move away from the table when he shows it. Do not move away…

He removed a cover from Cinzia's bowl.

"Oh," I said softly, looking at her food.

Not seafood.

The slave removed my cover. He placed it on the tray. I expected him to take it out of the room; however, he moved a couple of feet to Cinzia's right and then he went down to his knees, hands crossed behind the back of his ankle-length split skirt, and looked straight-ahead at the table.

"To frey," Cinzia said, pulling my attention to her. She held up her drinking glass to me.

"To frey," I said, lifting mine. She pressed her glass against mine and took a sip.

I took a sip.

I had just toasted to keeping men as slaves.

It was cold water. No weird taste.

I waited for her to lift her spoon. Then I took a bite of greintol.

"You like happy good?" she asked, on her third bite.

"Yes," I told her, honestly. I mean it was good. But it was hardly "special."

"You have food such like this on Earth?"

"Uh. Yes."

"What do you call it on English speak?" she asked, eager to learn a new English word.

Cinzia held her utensils carefully in each hand.

Maybe I had assumed they would be a bunch of hand-eating, teeth gnashing barbarians at the dinner table; so it surprised me that she was eating with more decorum than I did.

I adjusted my posture and tried to remember how Aunt Susan had taught me to eat at Sunday brunch.

"We call it 'scrambled eggs.' And, thank you. It is happy good."

* * * * *

The slave remained at Cinzia's side until we both finished eating. He cleaned the table and took our napkins and lap cloths.

He had turned to walk away when Cinzia suddenly told him to stop. He held fast.

Then she slapped his left buttock with a quick hit at his skirt!

He said something to her and then moved on with the dishes.

"That is Anrod," she said. "He has nice backs side, yes?"

"Uh. Yes," I replied.

True enough, he had nice shoulders and a strong-looking back.

But everyone was a bit smaller than humans. I mean, *Earth* humans.

At least I wasn't looking up at everybody here.

"We need more of bullets for raaa," she said. "I have mean to say: bullets for guns."

"Yes, I heard that before. Alexi's space wagon is not like mine. A Tamagra is loaded with bullets and guns and food. Rangers work for three or four months alone and have to carry a lot of stuff. But I did not load my space wagon with a lot of supplies. I'm only going to be here for another day."

"Sorry? You say another day?"

"Today and tomorrow."

"Then you bring us bullets?"

This seemed to be pretty important to them.

"Are you running out of bullets?" I asked.

She paused for a moment. "Running? Oh Sorry. We have not many now."

I raised the palm of my hands out to her. "Hold on, wait." I had to think about this.

A Tamagra would hold about a dozen different firearms. Add the built-in armament, and you had fifteen weapons. Two or three of them would be that rockin' new Crest-Leeland. It carried thousands of rounds because it had an unbelievable firing rate. Six cases of rounds for each of the other guns.

"There should have been around twenty-thousand rounds of ammunition on the Tamagra," I said.

"Sorry?"

I flipped open the pages of the dictionary. pointed to the numbers.

"Yes," Cinzia replied.

"Twenty-thousand," I said. She didn't understand the number.

"Yes," she nodded, enthusiastically

"Fucking twenty-thousand bullets? And you have used all of them?"

She looked at the page and pointed at a number. "Three of thousand bullets now."

They were pretty bad shots, or they had killed a hell of a lot of goddamned people.

"Wow," I said.

"Earth word," Cinzia said. "I know 'wow.'"

"I bet. Listen, uh, I'm not so sure about the bullets thing. This is pretty weird. We tell stories, not true stories, about finding other people on planets like this. But no one from Earth believes it will happen. So, uh, we." I grasped for the easy English words, but was not sure Cinzia was getting all of this. "We. I. I don't even know what to do about meeting you."

"We give you platinum. You give bullets. Happy good for all."

"Are you here with me just to negotiate?"

"Sorry?"

"Are you here to talk giving bullets?"

"No. Alexi say Earth people like to get angle on other Earth people. Erskan not like that. We talk 'straight up.'" She flashed her fingers in the air to imitate quotation marks.

It was comical and I almost laughed.

It would be as if an Australian aborigine had a conversation about thermonuclear dynamics while sitting around the camp fire over an evening of casual tribal drum beats.

"How much platinum do you have?" I asked, intrigued.

"We load fill all of your space wagon," she told me.

I laughed. "You need to be straight up with me."

She laughed. "I is straight up."

My smile must have faded.

Cinzia nodded.

A load of platinum, that big. . . It would be worth. Dear fucking god, that would be worth. . . I couldn't come up the number. Billions. Not a few billions. But seventy billion. Ninety billion. I could buy an Earth city.

"Okay, I am interested. First Alexi and Mermaid, then we talk business."

"'Mermak,'" she corrected me.

"Sorry," I told her.

Billions.

"Why is platinum good for Earth peoples?" Cinzia asked.

"Oh, a little history," I said. "The Earth Alliance of Democratic Nations, which we call 'Eaden' as a take-off of a biblical reference – never mind – was made by many different countries. Like the Erskan and Treaslok and Busai. They were mostly friendly. Then a team of scientists – uh, thinking people – learned a way to make a machine called a 'Corona Turbine.' This machine uses melted platinum, called 'Corona Oil,' to make it work. These scientists lived in a country called the Netherlands and a country called Japan. There was a big risk to take to spend the money, and another country called the United States gave the money to do it. The three countries made the Corona Turbine work and that allows us to go into space. They had exclusive rights to travel, and that means their language became popular."

I faced a blank stare.

"'Demo-scratch-it?'" she asked, stuck at the beginning.

Probably none of that made sense. At least I tried. "Uh, so what do you women do here while you are waiting to go fly over a castle?"

"Sorry? Oh, yes, sorry. What do we have to do fun?"

"Yes."

She snapped her fingers and rotated around, swiveling her boots to the floor and away from the table.

The man that had served our table ran over to her, dropped to his knees, and crossed his wrists behind his back.

I watched wide-eyed as she pushed his head down to her left boot. "Iz-ta brieneia," she told him.

She spread her boots slightly and leaned back, releasing her grasp on his hair.

He licked the top of her glossy black boot.

Laces ran up the front of her boot, criss-crossing over large silver pins, to just below her knee.

She looked at me and put her finger to her mouth as if to tell me "shhhh."

I nodded and watched, fascinated and repulsed at the same time.

His tongue continued to lick the inner side of her calf.

The handful of women in the room, seated at different tables, glanced occasionally in our direction but they were uninterested.

"Shra," she said.

The man reached her knee and began kissing her bare skin above the top of the boot.

He was moving slowly, kissing.

My feet moved involuntarily.

The slave kissed her inner thigh, reaching the point where the two-inch wide pleats of her purple-black leather skirt fell down between her legs.

When was she going to tell him to stop?

"Tar," she said.

He stopped and then kissed her left right boot. He sat back on his heels, still kneeling, and looked at the floor.

Cinzia took a deep breath. She had her eyes closed. Then she sighed.

"You want fun?" she asked, opening her eyes and looking at me.

I realized the drinking glass in my grasp was on the verge of shattering. I sat it on the table and consciously relaxed my fingers.

"No."

"Urja," she told him.

He kissed her boot again and stood. He glanced at me for only a moment, and then left the room.

His look was almost one of – disappointment?

"Yes, Jordan," she said. "Our frey want to serve you. They happy good about Earth woman here."

"Oh," I said.

"And, Alexi has make many frey friends. They are knowing you are – " she paused. "We have speak them that you are Alexi owner. We have no speak for a woman that has a frey but is not owner."

"No woman friends?" I said aloud.

She cocked her head.

"Nevermind."

"If Jordan uses other mind later, Jordan can ask and I have frey make pleasure for you."

That's what they did here for entertainment. I had a thought of my own: "I would be happy good to see the outside."

"Tural make ask that you have Erskan wearing if on the outside by the not warriors. This okay?"

I tried to put that together. Tural wants me to wear Erskan clothes if I'm outside by the civilians?

I *was* diggin' their outfits.

"You have a uniform that would fit me?"

"Yes!" she grinned.

"Okay. But only for tonight."

Chapter Three
Erskan Hospitality & Restraint

The door was shut behind me.

I looked around the rather large bedroom.

I figured a bedroom in a medieval castle would be all stone, with a hard thin bed, flaming torches on the walls, and a bear skin rug.

But this room was much nicer.

It even had a window view. I walked over to the window and pulled aside the decorative curtains and looked out.

The window panes were open, glass pulled to the side. The craftsmanship was amazing. Clean, straight edges around the metal frame. Everything was perfectly square.

I was eight floors high. There was a spacious field below, an inner perimeter wall – quite damaged – another field and wall. Several hundred horses were tied to posts in an area. Twenty or thirty women warriors were visible at any one time, mostly moving in pairs.

Beyond the outer gate were the rooftops of thousands of buildings. Chimneys poked out from rooftops of red, yellow, and black. Streets had died down, with only half of the people outside than I saw a couple of hours ago. It was still daylight, but the sun would be setting soon. It was probably dinner time.

I turned to the room.

Colorful tapestries lined the walls to obscure the stone walls and soften the room.

The bed was thick and comfortable-looking. It was plush with many pillows.

Several thick rugs lined the stone floor.

Candles and colorful floral arrangements covered several small tables.

The room had a woman's touch.

I moved closer to the bed and examined the headboard. Sturdy chains were permanently connected to the thick wood posts.

Okay, the room had an *Erskan* woman's touch.

Oh, the uniform.

I unlaced my combat-boots and then unzipped and removed the wrinkled flightsuit.

The Erskan uniform pants were made of heavy-weight black leather.

They had left a soft, silk-like thong for me.

I held it into the air. Rather small. But, okay, I pulled it on. It fit well.

I pulled the pants, tugging a bit to get it over my thighs.

It was the correct fit also. Rather snug, though.

I kept my own bra; then I dressed the white blouse around me and buttoned it.

There was enough of it to tuck into the pants. I fastened the pants with buttons – no zippers here – and then fed a wide leather belt around and buckled it.

My flight-style black boots did not match well, but they would do.

Finally I strapped my holster around my hip and made sure the StacGun was secure.

"Okay, Cinzia, ready," I said, opening the door.

She was on the other side of the hall talking with two younger uniformed women.

The three of them turned to face me.

"Something wrong?" I asked.

"Sorry?" Cinzia replied.

"You are looking at me."

"Happy good uniform," she said, nodding. "This is Onala," she pointed at one of the women. "Onala will be with on walk for us."

The youngest woman nodded to Cinzia and left the three of us.

"Howdy," Onala said. She was strong-looking for these smaller people. She had a StacGun holstered much like mine.

It was irritating to observe, but her custom-made holster looked to be of a better quality than what I used.

"Howdy," I replied, playing along.

She flashed a large smile and stepped back. So Onala would watch me.

"Please, after my walking," Cinzia told me, going ahead of me. I fell in behind her as Onala followed us.

* * * * *

44

"It was only three days that you beat the Treaslok people?" I asked.

Cinzia thought about my question. "Yes, three days."

"They do not appear to be mad at you."

"Corrigan and Ineer make bad times for Treaslok. Now Treaslok happy. Not happy good. But will be happy good."

"Ineer. She is an Earth woman?"

"We not knowing well. You have Tamagra outer?"

"Yes, I have a computer."

"Alexi say his puter would find Ineer. But not working."

"Where is the Tamagra?"

"It is in Antrana palace."

I stood to the edge of the sidewalk as several children, all female, ran past us.

Other adults moved along the walk. A few looked at Cinzia; none cared to notice me.

Onala watched everyone come near.

Then I noticed that she only paid attention to women that approached Cinzia; I was of a lesser concern.

"Should you be with Tural?"

Cinzia shook her head. "We have thinks that I could learn from Jordan."

"What is not working on the Tamagra? Do you know what happened?"

"Sorry, words are hard." She looked at her hands. Then raised one of them and lowered it to waist. "Alexi Tamagra on fire. Down goes into sand. Tamagra not working."

"What about Roberts?" I asked.

"Other Earth man?" She shook her head. "No alive. When Tamagra into sand."

I should try to recover his body.

"Can I see the Tamagra?"

"Yes."

That was a good answer; because I would see it. With or without their approval.

We stood in front of a ground-floor business. It appeared to a small grocery store. I glanced in the windows and saw several women moving around, carrying cloth bags stuffed with bread and other items.

"Not many slaves," I said, looking back to the street.

"Treaslok have less frey than Erskan. Erskan have. . . forty women and each frey. Treaslok have fifty women and each frey."

"Why is there such a bad number?"

I was starting to fall into a "baby speak" thing here.

"Alexi says gene... gene-etish." Frustrated, she raised her hands into the air. "You ask him."

There is that unidentified low-level radiation around the planet. Maybe that's doing something.

"I will. Yannow, I have to get back to my station in three days. If I'm gone longer than that they will send someone to look for me."

"Station know where you come to Aervanta?" Cinzia asked, snapping her head to me.

"Maybe. They know where, sort of. I filed a plan. I gave them a map."

Cinzia pressed her fingers her temple, "Arl! Follow please, me!"

I half-jogged to keep pace with her as we went back to the castle.

In less than two minutes we bounded the stairs, two at a time, until we reached their war room.

I sucked air; but Cinzia was barely winded as she called to Tural.

Too many soda waters; not enough cardio.

Tural sat at a table with several warriors nearby.

I rest my palms on my knees and tried not to draw too much attention to the fact that I was so out of shape. Comparatively speaking.

Tural and Cinzia exchanged several brisk sentences.

"Three days?" Tural asked. She got to her feet.

"I'm only staying here until tomorrow, anyhow," I told them. "Once we get Alexi back."

"You *not* bring more Earth people here," Tural told me.

It was not the most diplomatic way to put in a request.

"I'll bring anyone I need here to get Alexi," I told her, standing straight and looking into her eyes. "Anyone."

Nothing and nobody was going to get in my way. Queen or not.

Tural put her hands on her hips and glared at me.

"We can stick it to the plan," Cinzia offered as she stepped between us.

Tural abruptly sat down in her plushy chair.

She spoke to a seated uniformed warrior. The younger woman vacated the seat next to Tural and then pointed to the chair.

I moved toward them and sat down.

No one said anything for at least five seconds.

Tural and I locked eyes.

She may have fifty women in here, all armed with razor-sharp swords and several guns, but I wasn't going to change my mind just to make them feel better.

"Erskan wearing look happy good with you," Tural smiled, indicating my dress with her hands.

"Thank you."

"Jordan Sheri, you know why I not happy good with more Earth people?"

"Yes."

"What is we do to make that not happen?"

"Okay, here's what. Straight up. I want to get Alexi."

"Alexi is my frey," she said casually, as though it was a foregone conclusion.

I matched her matter-of-fact tone, "Well, we are going to have a problem, then."

Tural's smile faded. "Why problem?"

"Alexi is not a slave. And he does not belong here."

She processed what I said. Then, "Alexi is a true frey. He knows this. It is not Erskan make him true slave. He has slave in his heart and has Erskan to be here for him true selves."

"I don't think so."

"You will ask him," she offered, patting my knee. "Alexi tell you straight up true."

"You have make him tell me," I said. Fuck... I sounded like a Second Grader. "You have brain washed him."

"Sorry?"

"You make him tell me," I reverted back to child-speak.

"*You* will ask him," she said, sitting back. A smug smile formed on her face. She took a full drinking glass from a slave that knelt next to her chair. She sipped the red drink and handed the glass back to him. "Tell me, Jordan Sheri. What is you do when Alexi not want to go with you?"

I paused in my answer. In doing so, I gave away my real answer. That I frankly didn't have a fucking clue what to do about that.

I'd have to take him back home, against his will if necessary. Either way, he's going back to where he belongs.

"You take Alexi? Then you be taking him Makes you a trenama if you take someone that not wanting to go. Yes?"

"Maybe you are the trenama," I said.

Tural laughed.

"I am many things now. Trenama I am not. You will ask Alexi. He decides. Not you. Not I. Alexi."

"You make him stay," I told her.

"No. Alexi has one freedom of choice. Torino Primera has gave Alexi freedom to choose. I cannot take that freedom of choice. Only Alexi."

I nodded. "We find Alexi first."

"Yes." She patted my knee again, "I like Jordan Sheri. You and I want Alexi be happy good, yes?"

"Yes."

"Yes." She looked at the warriors about us. "You want go now to the space wagon?"

"Let's go find him," I said, placing my hands on my knees, part readying to stand and part to keep her from touching me again.

"Shia-talso," Tural said.

The warriors replied in another word and they stood to their feet.

I stood.

Tural took another sip from her drinking glass and handed it back to the man slave.

She looked up to me and nodded. "We go find him."

* * * * *

I waved my hand over the biometric scanner.

The door slid to the side.

"Watch your step," I warned Tural.

She climbed the metal steps into the spacer before the cockpit.

Cinzia, Onala, and a few other women came inside.

We had just loaded about eighty Erskan warriors, heavily armed, into the Number Two cargo hold.

"Liquid electricity," one woman beamed when she eyed the instruments.

"There are only three seats in here," I said, waving them to follow me to the cockpit proper. "Four of you will need to stand – but you can hang on to those straps there."

Cinzia translated.

The woman fascinated with the instruments spoke to Tural. It sounded as though she was pleading a point.

Tural nodded.

The woman dashed to the center seat and looked at me.

I pointed to the right seat.

I always drove on the left.

The woman plopped down into the right seat.

"Tell her not to touch anything," I advised Tural.

Tural did not speak, but looked at the woman instead.

"Uimisla," the woman said, smiling. She snapped the seatbelts around her like she had done it before. "I will not touch the navigation."

I shook my head. "How many people here speak English?" I wondered aloud, as I slid onto my seat.

"Alexi has taught me English. I am an engineer."

"You're the first Erskan that really seems to know English." I waved my hand over a few controls.

Tural sat in the middle seat.

"Pre flight," Uimisla commented.

Good thing the controls were electronic. I would have knocked a mechanical switch off the panel with my hand. "Yes, pre-flight. Very good."

Tural said something.

The woman laughed.

I stopped my pre-flight and looked at Cinzia.

Cinzia smiled at me and translated "Torino Tural say that Uimisla have sex pleasure and stick to the chair."

"I hope not. I'm only borrowing this thing."

Cinzia spoke in Erskan and translated what I said.

All of them laughed.

A few more controls to activate. "Okay, now, this is going to be very different than riding on the ground. You are –"

"Shia-talso," Tural interrupted.

"What's that?"

"'Go,'" Uimisla offered. "Just go."

Fine. I resisted the impulse to stab my finger onto the pressurization switch.

"Restraints," Uimisla pointed to me.

"Seat belts," I corrected. "They are not "restraints.""

And yes, I hadn't put mine on yet. I snapped the harness about my body.

I usually waited until the last moment.

Really.

The low-torque Corona drive began heating. We could hear popping sounds behind us.

The craft vibrated.

I activated the clearsteel screen.

Before us was the forest, darkened with nightfall.

I activated the forward lights.

The trees shone in brilliant clarity.

Tural spoke to Uimisla.

"Torino Tural demands – uh, requests, that you not use lights for now."

"Yannow, there is no way to turn off all of the lights. I can turn off the forward lights, but there are lights that will flash on the sides and bottom."

Tural understood most of my words. "Okay, we make good do."

"I'll cut the forward lights when we are in the air," I told them.

Tural retrieved her radio and was about to speak when I waved her to stop.

"Here, speak now," I said, after I activated the radio. "Tell everyone outside to get back."

She spoke aloud.

A woman's voice replied via the on-board radio speakers.

The lower left display indicated the riders and women had moved away from the ore hauler.

"Okay," Tural said. "Go."

"Hang on," I told them.

For an instant I contemplated giving my passengers a two-G sudden powerthrust lift. It would have really fucked with them.

Well, it might just encourage these women to make three-G's.

Instead, I made a gradual lift.

The craft pitched a bit as tree branches uncompressed.

None of the women flinched. They leaned forward to the clearsteel and intensely looked at everything.

I cut the front lights and dimmed the interior cockpit illumination.

With a wave of my hand the display changed to terrestrial-night mode. Topography was represented by closely-spaced green lines. Infrared and spectral sensors identified and separately illuminated other living objects.

Cinzia pointed at the artificial image of a small animal as it scurried away from us.

I increased vertical elevation to about a thousand feet.

The city came into view, the actual lights blended into the on-screen technical display. The sensors and display compensated and created an updated hybrid view.

Uimisla did appear on the brink of an orgasm.

I told them, "Let's avoid the city. We will go south, then very high, and cross the water. Then come around to the mountains."

I turned one-hundred eighty degrees and nudged the forward thrusters. In less than thirty seconds we were at twenty-thousand feet.

The Erskans blabbed in their language. They were pointing up, down, everywhere.

All of them were going to have one giant cum in my ship.

"Ladies," I said. "Amazons. Erskans. Whatever. Please, calm down." I made a right turn, banking heavily.

"See if they are okay back there," I suggested, after waving my fingers over the cargo switch.

Cinzia spoke aloud.

The reply was apparently positive.

"Happy good," Cinzia told me.

Cinzia laughed as the inertial dampeners failed to completely diminish the side-forces of the maneuver.

"You need to try an Earth ride called a 'roller coaster,'" I told her.

"With war on Treaslok over, now we Erskans can make ball bearings for civilian things," Uimisla said. "Alexi has drawn plans for a roller coaster."

"Goddam it," I said, partially under my breath. A goddamned roller coaster?

We skimmed over the sea and passed the Treaslok city on our right. I followed the coastline north.

"Uimisla, do you know what is wrong with the craft?" I asked, hoping she would know.

"Tamagra navigation computer fried up. Corona main fried up."

Good technical description.

"Seaport," Tural said, pointing to the bottom right.

It was a small seaport. Two ships were anchored.

We were already too close for us to avoid detection. I kept going straight on-course and flew directly overhead.

Cinzia snapped her radio to her face and rapidly spoke to it.

"We did not know of seaport. We send ships to it for attack," Uimisla explained.

"Hopefully they will not send a message to the mountain fortress," I thought aloud.

The three of them looked at me as though I were crazy.

"What?"

"Only Erskans have radio machines," Tural explained.

"You sure about that?" I asked.

That stifled their suggestions for a minute or two.

Ahead was the mountain range.

Elevation counters flickered on the display.

"Uh, wow. That's twenty-eight thousand feet high, at the peak," I said.

Uimisla spoke in Erskan language.

The women uttered surprise.

"Just how much English do you know?" I asked Uimisla.

"I know all the words in Alexi's dictionary. He writes English, I find hard Erskan words for him. I'm good with numbers and math. I am an engineer."

"I should have met you earlier today," I told her. "This would have made my day easier."

"Sorry. I was much busy in my skunk works working on a problem. Do you know chemical mix ratio for saltpeter and sulfur?"

I cocked my head at her.

Alexi, goddamn it!

Gunpowder?

Skunk works?

Was he helping them build a fusion reactor, too?

"No. I don't know how to make the stuff. Only how to shoot it."

I slowed to a stop. The thrusters whirred and strained to keep the ore hauler motionless. This would have been impossible if it was loaded with ore.

Or, perhaps, loaded with platinum.

On the south end of the mountain range, at merely two-thousand feet elevation from the ground were many graphic indicators of light and heat.

"That's probably it," I said.

"Happy good," Tural replied.

"We'll come from the east and hug the south side of that peak," I told them. "It should give us a bit of surprise."

We descended east and dropped to two-thousand feet. Then I turned us around and slowed to a ground speed of fifty miles per hour.

The terrain-following navigation system glided us between two mountains.

I slowed to twenty miles per hour.

"The mountain castle is around the next turn," I told them.

We came around the vertical ledge.

The display lit up: orange lines depicted the hard structure of the fortress.

Straight-edged stone extended from the mountain rock. Artificially-constructed walls stretched well over a hundred-feet high and overlooked a narrow road that snaked through the mountain.

A wide walkway lined the wall, which stretched a couple of hundred yards in length.

Inside the wall, half-built into the mountain and half stone-blocks, was the castle itself. Eight stories high. Two towers. Several inner-perimeter, low buildings.

I angled the pitch so that we could peer straight down into the courtyard.

"Do you want to drop right there?"

"No," Tural said. "We should make go quick. They see us now."

I activated the reverse thrusters.

A warning beep jarred me out of my skin.

"Erkak!" Uimisla huffed.

Another warning beep.

A section of the clearsteel display flashed bright red as it indicated a source of danger on the wall below.

"Netra!" Tural said and clutched her armrests.

"Warning," announced the ore hauler's female voice via the craft speaker.

"Fuck!" I shouted. I pulled hard on the controls and warned everyone, "Hold on!"

The ore hauler screeched in protest.

"Warning."

This old thing would only have an audible warning if there was an onboard fire or –

Our clearsteel view lit up like a fireworks show. Tracer fire and bullets rattled the cockpit.

I had to keep the front screen facing the attack or we were fucked!

The Erskans blabbered.

"Shut up!" I snapped.

"Warning."

A second section of clearsteel flashed bright red, to our right.

"Oh, fuck me!" I said. They had two guns.

I stomped on the foot controls and grit my teeth.

A line of tracer fire swept from the right. There was no way to deflect the gunfire from both weapons.

Retreat was the only way.

The ore hauler shrieked as the engines went to full reverse.

"Warning."

We backed away and I jerked the ore hauler around to make a run for the night sky.

I deactivated the audible warnings

A section of the clearsteel display provided a damage report.

Tural spoke with the warriors in the cargo hold.

"Okay," she said. "They okay."

I read the graphic again on the display.

"Oh, fuck me."

Uimisla looked at the display. Then she spoke to the Erskans.

"What is a Corona compensator?" Tural asked.

"It means this ship isn't going into space unless I can borrow one from the Tamagra."

Uimisla waved her hand at me.

"Yes?"

"Alexi has locked the inside of the Tamagra."

Goddamn it.

"Tural, do you know what it means to use a 'Plan B?'" I asked.

"Yes, Sheri Jordan. We use Plan C and Plan D much of all time. But it is Erskan letters, Plan Eta, Plan Ko, Plan D –"

I cut her off: "We must land this, and *now*. We can either put down by the big wall you talked about, or do it in the big yard by your Treaslok castle. Either way, we have to land in a few minutes to look at the damage."

"Dola," Tural said. "Land at the Treaslok castle." She lifted the radio to her mouth and spoke. A woman listened and replied in short answers.

After a moment the radio conversation was interrupted.

Another woman's voice came on, quick and pointed in her words.

At first Tural listened. Then Tural fired back.

They both paused.

The women in the craft held their breath while Tural stared at the radio.

The other woman made the funny Erskan laugh.

Then they made a cordial sound. Tural replaced the radio to her hip.

"Trouble?" I asked.

We were making our descent.

"No," Tural replied. She smiled and added, "Family."

"Ah, I understand."

The large field by the castle was more than suitable for landing the ore hauler. There would be plenty of room to spare – which was good because hundreds of women and several men were illuminated in the landing lights.

The craft came to rest. The landing struts rocked slightly as the thrusters faded.

"Happy good ride," Uimisla said. "Except for the gunfire."

"Yes. And thank you, all, for *not* telling me that the Treaslok have guns, too," I snapped.

I released the seatbelts and stood. I pointed to Uimisla. "You, come with me and let's look at the holes."

Chapter Four
Hunting North of KoVer

It wasn't too bad, really.

"These here," I pointed to several dents at the right side of the cargo hold.

Uimisla took her own Police flashlight and shone it on bullet impacts. "This is good Earth metal, yes?"

"Yes. But it was not made to take shots like that. Occasional meteor and orbital debris, maybe."

Uimisla blinked. "Mee tor?"

"Stuff...rocks that float in space. Small rocks."

She nodded, "Okay." Uimisla pressed her fingers onto the dents.

"My warriors thank you for fun ride," Tural said. She was flanked by Cinzia and a couple of other important-looking warrior women.

From a distance, two slaves hurried to assist, each carrying torches.

"Sure. We have to do it again." I pointed to a particularly deep dent, "What about that one?"

Uimisla pressed her finger against the body. "Not through and through."

"Right. But it may have damaged the Frictionlite. It's... nevermind. It could be a problem if I need to go fast. Catch the space wagon on fire."

There was the significant noise of people talking.

I turned to face Tural and her entourage. Several warriors stood with their back to us and formed a line around the ore hauler. This was because hundreds of women and a few men stood and pointed. And talked gibberish.

"This no secret now," Tural sighed. "All sees us land here. Big dance party."

"Sorry about that. You should have told me the Treaslok have guns."

"All Earth people have guns, yes?" Tural countered.

"No."

"Louis Corrigan is trenama because he takes guns and sells guns, yes?"

"Yes," I admitted.

"And you know this of Corrigan before you come to here?" Tural pressed.

"Yes."

"Then you know Corrigan have gun. Or two guns."

"Yannow, I'm not – " I said, about to tell her to fuck off. The damn problem with this was that she was right. "Yes, Torino Tural. Yes."

We looked at each other for several seconds.

"What is Plan D?" Tural asked.

"I was going to ask you that."

"Corrigan knows you have space wagon. That we have space wagon. He be ready on next time we go to his mountain place."

"Yes, I'm sure he will. Maybe Corrigan will have three guns to welcome us next time, too."

"Will space wagon fly?"

"It will fly here, yes. It will not go into space, up into very high sky. We have to get inside the Tamagra to get a part – a piece of the engine. To do that we need Alexi. And we only have three days."

Cinzia spoke to Tural.

Several of the Erskans spoke. I noticed that the Treaslok warrior was also in attendance, with a couple of similarly dressed women nearby. Big dance party.

The two sides seemed to be getting along well, considering the Erskans burned all their ships and wrecked their castle.

"Uimisla," I asked, "who are the Treasloks? What are their names?"

She looked away from the side of the body damage. "That is Monu. That is Lendon. They are learning to speak Erskan, but it will be some weeks until they can actually speak. Monu is fast learner. She was a... how is Earth word? Oh. What is Earth word? Big leader in army?"

"General?"

Her eyes brightened. "Yes. General. Erskan word is 'jurina.' Treaslok word is 'rijella.'" She pointed to Cinzia. "Cinzia is senior Korina Jurina. A big leader in Erskan army here. Only Tural is bigger leader."

I frowned. "Korina Jurina" must have been a special rank of a general, like a "brigadier general." It rhymed so much that it made me want to skip rope in the gym.

"Who was Tural talking to on the radio?"

"Oh. Wetana. Torino Primera Sklera."

"Wetana...that is her sister, yes?"

"Older sister of Tural. Sklera is leader of all Erskan and all Treaslok now."

"We would call her a 'queen,'" I told her. "Hell, you have some long names here."

"General George Smith Patton Junior," Uimisla said to me. "Now that is a long name."

"What?" I asked, snapping my head around. "Did Alexi talk about Patton?"

"He says from Earth history teachings he learned war-making strategy about General George Smith Patton —"

"Uimisla," Tural interrupted in her uneven English, "I have question about."

We both faced Tural and Cinzia.

Tural waved at the ore hauler with her hands. "Yiminee."

Uimisla twisted her lips. She turned her head and looked at the craft. Then she turned back to us. Her grin was plainly visible in the indirect light of several flashlights. She made the weird "oy oy oy" laugh.

"Yes?" Cinzia asked.

"Yes. I like it," Uimisla nodded.

Tural grinned.

"What?" I asked.

"You can ask Sheri Jordan if will work happy good," Tural offered.

"The space wagon can still fly over ground yes?" Uimisla asked.

"Yes. No problem there."

"Can you open the doors in the air?"

"Yes." I would need to manually reprogram several safety protocols. "Just tell me what you are planning."

* * * * *

I activated the pre-flight sequences.

Uimisla was in the middle seat. A young warrior was in the right seat, none-too-thrilled – at first. She clutched the arm rests.

"Lights," I said.

On the other hand, Uimisla was thrilled. She reached to the panel and swept her fingers over the forward lighting control.

The area ahead was flooded with artificial daylight.

Hundreds of women actually stepped back a foot or two, surprised.

"Tural, we are ready to go," I spoke aloud.

"Our warriors will okay to be ready good in one hour," her voice came back on the in-ship speakers.

"Okay."

"Shia-talso," Tural told us.

I thought a half-hearted attempt to reply in-kind would sound, well, half-hearted. So I didn't try.

But Uimisla turned to face me.

"Shia. Talso," she whispered, spreading the words out.

"Shia. Talso," I replied, loudly.

It could have meant "Kill the space invader later."

I activated the thrusters and began a slow vertical ascent.

From above we could see several hundred warriors forming into rows. More were flowing into the castle yard from a couple of roads. Flaming torches lit up multiple inbound roads.

I turned west and increased altitude to five-thousand feet. Then I applied forward thrust.

The string of little moons cast a unique and cool reflection on the sea. It was certainly easy to figure out which way was north or south or east; one only had to look into the sky.

Uimisla spoke to the young warrior, and excitedly pointed to the sea, to the moons, to the few clouds.

But the young warrior wasn't having a good time.

At eight-hundred miles per hour it only took us about fifteen minutes to cross the sea. Uimisla saw the velocity indicators. Her face was like a dog hanging out a moving car window.

"Follow that desert," she said, pointing to the green topography display.

I decelerated to six-hundred miles per hour and dropped to a thousand-feet.

"What are we looking for?"

"Two buildings."

After twenty minutes the scanners detected the first structures.

"Turn north, to the right, and go twenty miles, then stop," Uimisla said.

The young woman spoke to Uimisla.

Uimisla replied in a reassuring voice.

"She knows this place well."

"What's it called?"

"KoVer. It is south of here."

I turned north and decelerated to a crawl.

"Pretty dark out here," I said. "Are you sure these are going to come over?"

"Lower," Uimisla told me.

I dropped us to about twenty feet above the perfectly flat desert surface.

The display detected nothing.

Blue and red strobe lights flickered around us, reflecting from the hard, sun-baked mud below.

"Open the doors," Uimisla said.

I cycled the switches.

Six cargo hold doors opened per side. An electronic display indicated full open status.

"Now, lights."

"Okay." I activated all of the lights on the craft. This included the in-hold lights. Also, when you consider that an ore hauler is used in dust-blown environments you realize that the lights had to be extremely powerful. Those exterior lights cast a beam for a half-mile around us.

"When are –" I said, but abruptly ended my question.

The display indicated several red dots at a distance.

After five seconds the dots were joined into short dashed lines.

After ten seconds more there were thick red lines approaching our position.

From all around us.

"Goddamn," I huffed.

"We are much high and safe now," Uimisla said. She smiled. "Wait."

I looked beyond the electronic display and through the actual clearsteel window. A hazy-brown fog was moving in.

"Goddamn," I repeated.

"Yiminee," Uimisla laughed.

The young warrior unsnapped her seat belt and indicated she would get up; however Uimisla reached out and pressed her palm downward against the frightened woman's shoulder.

The donut-shaped swarm advanced at an amazingly high rate of speed. I began estimating when they would arrive when – they did!

They collided below us.

I leaned to the center of the floor and looked through the floor-panel.

"Holy Christ," I exclaimed.

"Now we go lower a bit," Uimisla told me.

"Yeah. A bit."

I dropped a foot. Then a couple more.

I looked to the left. The swarm was about four feet off the ground. I lowered the ore hauler until the bottom of the cargo holds were just barely below the top of the swarm.

Display indicators flashed.

"Filling up," I commented.

The young warrior stared at the display, fascinated by the view.

"Here, this is cool." I activated a section of her viewscreen and pulled in a live-video feed from Cargo Hold Three.

Millions of buzzing insects crowded the hold. In fact, they obscured the view after a few more seconds.

I dropped another six inches.

"Think that's enough?" I asked.

"Are we full?" Uimisla wondered.

"I have no idea. Carrying a billion bugs wasn't in the flight training class."

"Want to go look by self person?" Uimisla asked.

"Not really. No."

She nodded. "I agree. We are full then."

I closed the doors.

Then I cut the exterior lights.

"Okay, here we go."

We rose to five-thousand feet and reached eight-hundred miles per hour.

"Tural, this is Jordan, over."

"Jordan, please speak, gova."

"We have the bugs. Are you ready?"

"Two-thousand warriors are ready."

"Good." I looked at the navigation display and made a course correction. "Thirty minutes until we drop our little meat-eating bugs and then come pick up you and your warriors."

"Good."

"Tural. You better be right about Alexi. That he's not outside."

There was a pause.

Then she spoke: "It will be morning. They will have him locked in the dungeon."

The navigation system targeted the mountain castle. Flight path indicators were superimposed over the terrain below.

"In this case, I do hope he is in a dungeon," I said.

"Tural, gova," she said.

"Jordan, out," I answered.

Twenty-nine minutes.

Alexi, goddamn it, you better be indoors.

The sun peeked from the eastern horizon as we screamed toward our target.

Chapter Five
Fortress of Pain

The worst part about it was the bone-chilling cold.

Not the whipping. In some ways, Tural's fondness for whips had increased my tolerance to that type of pain.

Not the slapping. Tural had slapped me a few times.

Not the –

My teeth chattered and I lost my thought.

My hands shook and rattled the chains.

The cell was small. Five feet by five.

A single chain was connected to the metal ceiling bars. It hung down until eight inches above the cold stone floor. Wide metal wrist manacles were locked upon me and to the chain. It elevated my arms slightly, just enough to make it uncomfortable, and enough to cause my hands to lose blood circulation.

But it was so cold!

I had a blanket below me and one blanket on top of me. But my hands were exposed. Worse, the chain seemed to channel the cold temperature directly to my wrists.

It was no more than fifty degrees in the cramped cell.

And it was completely black.

I curled my legs into my body and tried to keep the heat close to me. The ankle manacles and the short connecting chain clinked.

Three nights? Five? I lost track. This had become my home when they weren't torturing me. At least in here I wasn't getting my ass beat.

I knew it was coming close, though.

Too soon.

That bitch, Ineer. She was as bad as the Treasloks.

Corrigan just watched. Smiling. He never raised a hand at me.

It probably had something to do with an agreement – to not have a man strike another man.

There was a big difference about the torture.

My Tural, she would torture me until I couldn't stand it. She knew how to push me to endure to a limit. Then she would go just a little bit further and stop. Then she would take me down and hold me until...

The Treasloks...they did not stop.

Yesterday morning, I was whipped to the point of passing out. I woke up later and found that they had continued to whip my body.

I did not believe Corrigan. Tural was not killed in the invasion. He is lying. She would never give up on me. She –

The door lock rattled.

"Out!" the woman's voice, in coarse English, ordered.

I squeezed my eyes at the light from the hallway.

She kicked my legs.

"Aah!" I exclaimed. Her boots hit my shins.

"Out!" she shouted.

I got to my knees and held out my wrists.

The blanket fell off my shoulders.

My body shook.

I was so cold.

There were always three guards. Two of them came in and surrounded my whipped and beaten body as the first guard unlocked the manacles from the ceiling chain. The wrists were chained to the ankle chain.

They reached under my arms and lifted me to my feet.

Then I was shoved out of my tiny dark cell.

Two guards dragged Mermak from his cell. He looked horrible. Hundreds of welts ringed his naked body. He coughed several times, a deep raspy sound. He would catch pneumonia in here – we both would.

Glassy eyes looked at me. He was becoming ill.

The guard on my right threw a punch at my stomach.

I doubled over in pain, my vision blacking out for a few seconds.

Tears streamed down my face.

They grabbed my arms and forced me to climb the stairs.

The Treaslok guards were dressed in their heavyweight uniforms to protect them from the cold mountain air.

They dragged us outside to the main courtyard. Traces of ice lined the torch-lit wall.

This would be the first whipping of the day. Followed by the late-morning whipping before bread and water. Followed by the afternoon whipping. Bread and water. And then the evening whipping. Four times a day. For five days. Eight days?

Corrigan and Ineer never asked a question of us.

Mermak and I both shivered violently as they dragged us to the center of the yard.

There were eight wide-diameter wood posts sunk into the stone. Each pillory was twenty feet apart from one another. They formed a wide circle.

I was pushed up against the ice-cold wood. My wrists were unlocked and then dragged tightly around the post and locked.

My ankles were unlocked and then also pulled wide apart.

As I had to do each morning, I relieved myself by urinating on the post. It was better to do it outside than in the little dark cell.

I heard Corrigan laugh behind me.

I was unable to turn my head far enough to see.

He would be sitting on a chair, sipping hot rita-bean broth. Ineer would stand next to him with her equally evil smile.

I could look up, and I saw a little brightness on the top of the mountain. The sun would be up in a minute or two.

Every sunrise gave me hope.

Mermak was chained to the pillory.

He looked really bad.

I had said nothing to the Treaslok. On the first day they said that I would have my tongue cut out if I spoke. I knew it was not a hollow threat.

But Mermak would die if he did not get some warmth and food soon.

The two Treaslok guards behind me laughed. Then they spit on my back and in my hair.

I knew the whip would be next.

The two Treaslok whip mistresses were flawless in their skill.

I heard the whip whistle in the air to my left. Mermak would be first.

It cracked, wrapped around the wood pillory, and then cut into his exposed body.

He screamed.

Then I heard it sailing in the air for me.

My thighs were on fire!

The whip seared into my legs, and burned them to the core.

I howled, uncontrollably.

The other whip cracked. Mermak shrieked.

The whip behind me snapped in the air once, to my right.

I flinched. My entire body shook violently.

She toyed with me, the miss intentional.

Tears streamed down my face.

My vision was blurred.

I tried to lick my lips.

But they were dry.

I had nothing to drink since yesterday afternoon.

The long whip wrapped around the pillory and snapped at the middle of my back.

My body jerked and I screamed, spit frothing at my lips.

My legs collapsed; but I was hung up by my wrists.

The metal cuffs cut into my wrists; but I did not care.

Crack!

Mermak howled.

My legs were whipped. I jerked on my wrists, uselessly trying to move. Anywhere. Somewhere.

The wood pole was ice cold and my feet were freezing to the stones. They were numb.

If only my body was numb.

Crack!

Mermak whimpered.

I looked at him. My eyes tried to focus.

He was limp, his head hanging backward, neck outstretched.

Streaks of blood covered his back.

"Hital!" a woman's voice announced behind me. It was the Treaslok word for "stop."

I clenched my teeth, readying for another hit.

Instead two Treaslok guards approached Mermak.

He was unconscious.

One guard pressed his eyelids up while another felt his neck.

"He is not awake now," one of the two guards said.

The leader of the guards – I never heard her name – walked behind me. She pulled my hair and forced me to look at her.

"Now you take your strikes and his strikes."

I did not bother to shake my head or protest. It would be useless.

She spit into my face.

It rolled off my right cheek and down to my neck.

Around her, I saw that Ineer had moved over to Mermak and the two guards.

She was a tall Earth woman. Short-cut black hair, not so attractive, rather rough-looking. I figured she was on parole or an escapee at least.

"Is he dead?" she asked in English.

"No, Lady Ineer," one of the guards replied.

"The Ranger will take his whips. So take him down to his cell. We'll see him again before I have my lunch."

She noticed that I looked at her.

The two guards unlocked Mermak's ankles.

Ineer walked toward me. She had a big smile.

"You can have another blanket if you can stay conscious through another twenty strikes. But you only made it through ten strikes last night. I don't think you can stand twenty this morning. And that's a shame." Ineer rubbed her gloved hands on her thick leather coat. "It appears to be cold outside."

The guards released Mermak's wrists and turned him around.

And then he did something that made my heart stop.

He ran!

He headed to the closest wall.

The two guards, surprised, chased after him.

Mermak was going to jump.

He closed within twenty feet of the wall, his feet staggering.

He wouldn't make it.

He got within five feet of the wall when one of the guards struck at his ankles with a whip.

Mermak tumbled onto the stone and came to a stop at the base of the wall.

I wasn't sure he would have even had the strength to pull himself up the three-foot ledge and then jump over.

But it did not matter.

They caught him.

"That's interesting," Ineer said.

I heard Corrigan laugh behind me.

The Treaslok guards kicked and beat Mermak. He rolled into a ball, sobbing.

Sunlight reflected off the snow-covered peaks of the mountains around us.

Mermak was bathed in light as they continued to kick him.

Blood covered the stones.

I tensed. They were going to kill him.

Ineer walked away from me and over to them.

She raised her hand and spoke in Treaslok to the guards.

They stopped kicking Mermak.

He was rolled onto his stomach. The ankle cuffs were secured with the short chain again.

Ineer spoke to them again.

Another guard walked over.

The three of them grabbed onto Mermak's arms and dragged him from the courtyard. I watched his ankles scrape the stone. Blood trailed behind him.

They pulled him into the building and shut the heavy wood door.

Ineer walked back to me.

"Do you want to jump? I can let you go now. You can jump."

I did not answer.

"You are permitted to answer me. One word only."

"No," I whispered.

"You tell him later, that if he commits suicide, that I will kill you by dissection. Nobody dies unless I say so."

She stepped back.

"Twenty, now, quickly. I want to see him bleed."

I looked across the courtyard and upward to the towers of the castle. There were several windows, including one that opened to a large room that frequently held numerous women observers.

Because they usually held cups or ate food I assumed it was a banquet hall or –

The whip cracked and my thighs exploded.

I screamed.

Before I could get my breath, I was hit around my legs again.

I was unable to make a sound.

The whip tore into my thighs again.

It burned. And I knew I had been cut this time.

My eyes were shut but they were white-hot with agony as the whip sliced my thighs again.

It had to end.

I just had to hold on until I got back into my cell.

It was cold there.

But I wasn't beaten.

The whip cut my legs.

I tried to scream. But I felt dizzy.

Then I fell into a pit of red.

Chapter Six
Special Delivery

"We are approaching the target," I told Tural. "Sixty seconds until our first pass."

"It is too bright," Uimisla said.

"They won't have a chance to shoot at us," I reminded her.

"We is ready for you and space wagon," Tural replied.

I eyed the control that would open the cargo doors.

"This will put us about five-hundred feet above them," I said, adjusting our altitude.

I made the final course correction.

The navigation system had recorded the terrain around the mountain castle and I had pre-plotted our approach, attack, and return to the Treaslok castle.

Our speed was at one-hundred miles per hour.

"Here we go," I told Uimisla.

The young warrior had released her grasp on the armrests and was now intent on watching everything.

We banked to the left.

The castle was only a thousand feet ahead.

It was early morning. Sections of the castle were illuminated by reflections. Others were still dark.

Snow lined the shaded walls.

I reduced speed to fifty miles per hour.

Several women lined the enemy walls at regular intervals. Most did not notice us.

I slowed to ten miles per hour and released the locks on the cargo holds.

There were perhaps fifty, sixty women visible below us throughout the courtyard and walls.

The clearsteel display indicated that our "cargo" fell out.

"One is running toward us with a firearm!" the young warrior said. She pointed to our right.

"That's okay," I told her. "We're almost... okay, done!"

My right hand shoved the acceleration control to maximum.

We made a hard vertical ascent, while rotating one-hundred eighty degrees.

Uimisla leaned over her seat and looked through the floor clearsteel panel.

A gray-brown cloud fell below us.

We continued our ascent.

I stopped at one-thousand feet above the castle.

The gray-brown cloud thinned, spreading wider below us, and quickly obscured our view of the castle grounds.

"Is it working?" Uimisla asked.

"Nobody is shooting at us," I replied, looking down also.

We couldn't see anything in particular. The yiminee bugs were concentrated between us and the castle.

"Time to go," I said. We climbed another thousand feet and I maneuvered through the mountain peaks. "Tural, this is Jordan. Cargo delivered. En route to your location."

"Understood."

We broke through the mountain range and flew over expansive rolling hills of green.

I looked at the video feed. No bugs. I swept my hand over the controls to shut the cargo doors and increased speed.

The Treaslok city, Dola, was highlighted on the center display.

I had the ore hauler pegged. We were moving at over a thousand miles per hour. It was critical we put our warriors on the ground soon after the bugs had done their damage.

The craft vibrated and rocked as I made the approach on the north side of the city.

"There!" Uimisla pointed.

"Got it," I nodded.

The display indicated a large number of people on the ground.

I cut the speed and set in for the landing.

Breaking thrusters rattled the craft.

It was impressive; two-thousand warriors on the ground remained in a tight formation and were absolutely rigid in their position when I landed between the two groups.

We skidded to a stop on the thick grass.

I opened the rear-most cargo doors, two on either side.

I looked from side-to-side. Tural was on the left side of the craft. She pointed at the doors. Other warriors raised arms.

Hundreds of Erskan and many Treaslok women ran to the two cargo holds and jumped inside.

On my right was Cinzia. She directed a similar operation.

Ahead were three warriors, watching both sides proceed.

"Damn," I said.

"What is wrong?" Uimisla asked.

"Amazing. Very efficient."

"Yes, we are," she flashed white, even teeth.

The last of the women warriors filed into the cargo holds. Tural waved to the women at the front of the craft with a series of hand signals. They replied.

Tural looked my way and pointed up.

Then she jumped into the cargo hold.

Cinzia repeated the commands and then entered the ore hauler.

One of the women in front of us raised both hands to her shoulders and then pointed her fingertips skyward.

Uimisla looked at the video feeds. "Happy good."

I closed the doors.

"Back to the mountain castle," I said.

Within thirty seconds we screamed over the hills.

The mountain range filled our view.

"We are too big to land," Uimisla said.

"Yeah, I know. Plan 'E.'"

"Oy, oy, oy," Uimisla laughed. "We should use Erskan language now. More letters than are in the English."

We split the first of the mountain peaks.

The sun was now solidly above the horizon, though dark shadows were cast onto the castle.

"Look!" Uimisla exclaimed.

There was a low gray-brown haze on the courtyard; not nearly as thick as before.

Several objects were visible. People.

Parts of people, actually.

"This is going to be tricky," I said. I flipped the audio controls. "Tell them there will be a few hard bumps before we open the doors."

Uimisla gave the warning.

I dropped down to the same elevation as the closest wall that lined the courtyard.

The nose of our ore hauler was two-thousand feet distant from the wall and the swarm of insects.

There was a four-foot high cloud of the yiminee bugs. They were walled-in and filled the courtyard.

"None of you mother fuckers shooting at me now," I said.

But we could not land in there either.

I moved us to within a thousand feet of the wall. "Plan E."

I brought the ore hauler about and spun it on the axis.

Uimisla realized what was about to happen. She grabbed onto the arm rests.

The young warrior clutched her own chair.

"Prepare for impact!" I said.

"Hoka dei ara brei, gliria!" Uimisla translated to the warriors in the back.

The right rear of the ore hauler crashed into the stone wall.

We were jarred.

Status indicator lights flashed on our displays.

I activated the rear-view video. The rear of the ore hauler had broken twenty-feet past the wall and into the courtyard.

"Here's the tricky part," I told Uimisla.

I simultaneously activated the forward thrusters and the main rear engines.

The ore hauler vibrated.

More warnings scrolled on the displays.

"Get ready to jump," I told Uimisla.

"Hoka dei sooma erko!" Uimisla repeated.

That burst of thrust should have cooked most of the bugs – and anything else in the courtyard for that matter.

I eased off the rear engines and we gradually moved in reverse until I had one-hundred feet of the rear of our craft over the ground. Then I cut all lateral thrust and let the cargo hauler float above the surface.

"Can we go to the land?" Uimisla asked.

I opened the doors.

"No. Too heavy. This might crush the castle."

One-thousand, five-hundred Erskan and Treaslok warriors streamed from the cargo holds.

There were no visible swarms of bugs.

"We are exited," Tural's voice announced over the radio.

I applied gradual thrust and moved away from the castle. I closed the doors.

A number of ten-foot by ten-foot stone blocks tumbled off the edge of the wall as we broke free.

The audio system jarred my ears, 'Warning."

"Tural!" I shouted. "Gun! Up high on the inside tower."

I engaged the lateral thrusters.

Display indicators flashed – we were being hit from above, at the rear-section of the ore hauler.

Then it stopped.

"Killed it," Tural replied. I heard shouting and the clash of metal about her voice.

"Good. Okay, we are headed to the next stop."

We banked to the right and I put us into a gradual descent, and aimed for the lowest, level surface of the narrow mountain road.

"Tel them to get ready," I told Uimisla.

She translated the notice.

After a minute we were at the bottom of the road, at least a mile's hard march upward to the castle. I landed on the ground and flattened a massive area of low shrubs and plants.

"Door opened," I said.

The remaining five-hundred warriors jumped from the middle cargo doors.

We watched as they quickly organized.

They began a fast march up the road.

I wanted to go – but someone had to provide air support. And that person was, unfortunately, me.

"You want to fight," Uimisla noticed.

"Yes, I do."

She cocked her head slightly. "You not live long in this battle."

"Thanks for your vote of confidence." I paused, "And you?"

"I am warrior first, engineer second."

"Oh?"

"I have combat practice on each two days."

"Does that mean you are good?" I asked. I looked at her. She was a little younger than I, a little thinner, but she had solid-looking biceps and defined shoulders. I added, "I'm not challenging you. Just asking."

"Twenty-six deaths. I think not bad."

"Oh." I had only shot and killed two people.

"You?" she asked.

"How many women do you think were up there when we dropped the bugs and then I used the engines?" I asked.

"Fifty?" she offered.

"Fifty-two," I said.

"Then I think you not bad either now."

That might have been a compliment.

"Now we wait, like happy peas in a Earth pod," Uimisla said.

Chapter Seven
Searching for Survivors - I

"Tural, my hand!" Virada shouted to me.

I jumped clear of the Earth space wagon.

Visada took my hand and pulled me behind her shield.

Several crossbow bolts pelted the steel shield.

There was gun fire.

I peered around the shield and looked up.

"There!" Visada said.

I pointed to one of our snipers.

Jordan Sheri shouted to us from Visada's radio. It was so fast I could not understand her English.

Our sniper fired a shot at a Treaslok sniper above and to our left.

Treaslok Loyalists attempted to bar the doors leading from the courtyard to the inner building.

"Dead!" Visada told me.

"Killed it!" I shouted to Jordan Sheri.

But other Loyalists fired hundreds of bolts down into our positions.

"They have rapid fire crossbow guns!" Visada said.

Cinzia's voice came over Visada's radio. "Tural, we have broken through here!"

I raised my head above the shield.

On our right, across the eight-hundred foot wide courtyard, Cinzia's force pressed into the west tower. They streamed into a ground-level double door.

On our left, closest to the east tower, were our forces. Erskan warriors and Treasloks. The Treasloks wore double blue and red cloth strips tied to their waist and right bicep.

We were pinned down.

"Take out those crossbows!" I told the sniper.

She nodded, crouching between two shields.

Eight large tree stumps were near us, in the middle of the courtyard, burned to a crisp.

Several clumps of charred bones and flesh lay scattered next to the trees.

There were pieces of metal cuffs and chain strewn about.

A crossbow bolt hit my shield.

"Netra! Get them!" I shouted to the sniper.

At least a hundred of Cinzia's forces penetrated the inner wall.

A series of hand signals were relayed to Visada under the cover of the shields that we held overhead.

"We have broken the door on our side," she told me.

"Attack," I nodded.

She flashed hand signals in return.

Our forces began to move toward the door.

The crossbow bolts stopped.

"Three," the sniper told me, a satisfied grin on her face. "I took three down."

I flashed a smile at her and then ran past.

We burst past the gate and into the castle.

The bodies of several dozen Loyalists, a few Erskans, and a few Treaslok lay on the floors.

Blood was splattered on the walls and floor – even the ceiling dripped crimson.

The sound of fighting was all around us, echoing off the stone walls.

Peto moved our way, pressing past Erskan and Treaslok women.

"There are more than a thousand Loyalists here," she huffed.

Her uniform was blood stained.

"Our estimate of a thousand total was incorrect," I realized. I grabbed the radio, "Cinzia! We are outnumbered here. Situation report!"

Monu replied, "Outnumbered as well. We are moving forward. Cinzia is fighting. Okay!"

I made a step toward the hall, toward the sounds of fighting.

Visada put her hand in front of me. "No, Torino."

"Arl!" I exclaimed.

I wanted to find Alexi and Mermak.

And then I wanted Corrigan.

"Get me a prisoner," I told Visada. "I want to know where the dungeons are."

She nodded and ran forward.

Peto stood by my side, catching her breath. "I killed four," she said, as an afterthought. Perhaps she was trying to justify taking a break.

I knew that the halls would be crowded and having too many fighters in one area was ineffective.

"Okay," she said, straightening. "Three more to go."

Peto turned and jogged toward the fighting

Fem Fist Books

Chapter Eight
Searching for Survivors – II

I regained consciousness.

Two Treaslok guards dragged me by my armpits, my back facing downward.

My heels painfully scraped the stone floor – that is what probably woke me.

I kept my chin pressed to my chest, though. Then I peeked through my left eye.

We were near the lower levels, deep into the natural rock of the castle. Close to the dungeons and my small frozen cell.

In another minute or two there would be no escape.

We reached the first and only check-point.

A single guard sat on a stool, stationed at the wide, metal-reinforced wood door.

She got to her feet and produced the keys to the lock.

Mermak would not survive another day.

And I became weaker every hour.

It was now.

Or never.

The door guard turned her back to us as she inserted the key.

My wrists were manacled before me with a one-foot long chain.

My ankles were manacled together.

My only concern was whether my tortured thighs would support my own weight.

I closed both eyes and visualized my plan of attack.

The locking mechanism in the door clicked. That meant the key was fully inserted and the door guard's attention was divided.

I pressed my feet to the floor and brought my hands together, effectively locking the hands of the two guards under my arms.

They both reacted by trying to pull apart.

I let them do so.

They let go and I fell.

But I turned and swept my legs to the right.

The metal cuffs caught the outside knee of the guard on the right. She buckled and went down.

The guard on the left reached for her club.

Our hands locked on it.

Even though I was in pretty bad shape, my upper body strength was superior. I ripped the club from her hands and rolled it back, over her own forearm.

Then I shoved it up into her windpipe.

She wheezed as her throat collapsed.

The guard at the door had rotated around and reached for her own club.

I struck back, to my right with the club, and nailed the first guard at her chest. It was a light, disorienting strike.

She fell against the wall.

I dove into the door guard.

Our clubs intersected in the air.

I was stronger than she and pushed her down.

Then I got one hit at the top of her head.

That was enough to slow her.

I got three more impacts until her eyes rolled into her head.

The first guard attempted to stand.

I grabbed the club out of the limp hand of the door guard and threw it, spinning end-over-end, to the head of the first guard.

The club hit her solidly on the forehead.

I was upon her in an instant. My fists pounded her head with several strikes.

The second guard sat on the floor, gasping, both hands around her injured throat. Her wheezing noise grated on my nerves.

I got to my feet and reached into her purse. My fingers found a key.

"I wish your clothes would fit," I said, in English.

I unlocked the ankle manacles. I had never realized before coming to this world that ankle manacles were effective because they cut into the Achilles tendon – it was hard to walk slowly, much less attempt a full-out attempt to flee. I breathed out in satisfaction as the last of the two thick metal cuffs fell from my feet.

The guard tried to back away, moving her body against the wall.

"No, I don't think so."

I walked over to her and wrapped my wrists and chain around her neck.

"A year ago I would have never done something like this," I said. "But."

I jerked the chain and my wrists.

Her neck snapped and she slumped. Dead.

I unwrapped the chain and performed the same execution on the other two.

There would be no suddenly-they-come-back-and-kill me thing happening here.

I unlocked my wrists, but used the chain to drag their bodies into the dungeon.

Then I collected the clubs and found Mermak's cell.

"Mermak? It's Alexi. I'm coming in."

I unlocked the door and entered the cell.

Mermak was curled into a ball, shivering.

He did not have a single blanket.

I crouched next to him and unlocked the ceiling chain.

He rolled over.

"Alexi?"

"Yes."

"Is Cinzia here?"

"No. No one is here. But I am getting us out."

"What did you do?"

"I killed three of them."

He forced a half smile. "Good."

I unlocked the rest of his chains and manacles.

"Hang on."

I walked around to get a blanket from my cell.

It was empty. No blankets.

"Sorry, man. I was going to get a blanket for you." I sat next to him.

Mermak's body was covered with skin cuts and angry red and purple welts.

I looked at my legs. So was I.

Mermak lifted his head up and put it on my thigh.

I ran my hands through his hair. "Mermak. We have to get out of here."

"I cannot."

"Yes, you can."

Tears ran down his face.

"Can you walk?" I asked.

"Yes, I think so."

"Then we need to go. I don't know when the guards will do their rounds."

"I -- I am ashamed," he finally confided.

"What? About running to the wall?"

"I tried to kill myself. I am a coward."

"Mermak. You and I both know you are not a coward. What they are doing here – that's torture. True torture and abuse. They want to break your mind. And it makes you do things that are not smart."

"You are still smart," he said.

I cradled his head like he was a wounded animal.

"Mermak, your people here, on Aervanta, for all of your fighting and the sadomasochistic culture that you are, you still are a people that don't have vicious crime and horrific abuse. You haven't seen anyone do this. But I have. I've seen victims of violent crime and I know what people can do to other people. I'm just telling you that I know what this is, and I understand it. Because I understand it, I am better prepared for it."

"I cannot face Cinzia."

"What happened this morning is something only you and I will ever know. Right?"

He nodded.

"We need to go."

Mermak sat upright with a groan.

He looked at my legs and gasped.

"Yeah, I probably need thread and a needle for two or three of these." I stood and helped him to his feet. I handed a club to him, "It's not going to do much against a sword, but. . ."

He took it. "I have never struck a woman before."

"Today's your day," I said, walking out of the cell. "Now, quiet."

He followed me to the door. It looked clear and we went through.

We came to an intersection, dimly lit by torches.

All of our visits to the surface had been to the route on the left. We turned right and moved quickly along the hall.

And we stumbled directly onto a fully-armed Treaslok warrior.

She was, however, staggering and nearly fell into me.

I raised the club and snapped a shot at the back of her head as she went down to the stone.

Mermak stared, wide-eyed. "My heart stopped," he whispered.

His Mistress said something like that all the time. I grinned at him.

I rolled the Treaslok's body over.

Her face was torn in many places. Blood soaked her uniform. An eye was missing. Her left ear was partially chewed off.

And her hands looked like they had been stuck in a meat grinder.

"What the hell?" I asked, confused.

Mermak unsheathed the dead woman's sword. He handed it to me.

"This is going to be as useful against them as holding a toothpick would be," I said to him. A skilled warrior would cut me into pieces without blinking.

The sword was heavier than I thought it would be.

"Have you ever used a sword?" he asked, hopeful.

"No. Have you?" I waved it about, feeling the handle.

"No. It is forbidden."

"Looks like a stupid law now, doesn't it?" I said.

"Yes."

"We have to talk to our Jurinas about changing that," I told him. "Okay, let's keep going. That way."

Chapter Nine
Searching for Survivors – III

"Torino," Visada called to me.

I looked over my shoulder. Two of the kuretno officers stopped talking as Visada ran to us.

We had cleared and secured the ground floor, the first lower-level floor, and the first above-ground floor. We had engaged in fighting on a wide, sweeping staircase that span from the ground-floor to the upper-most sixth floor.

"Yes?"

"Peto received information a few minutes ago about the dungeon location."

I could see Peto's back as she waited to engage in the fight. "Bring Peto to me," I told an Erskan officer.

I waited a few seconds until Peto arrived.

"Where is the dungeon?"

"Down one level there is the large entry hall we came in. We didn't go right because it heads to Cinzia. But we have secured the entry. But if we go farther there is a set of doors that lead to stairs. Straight down four floors. Direct to the dungeon."

I stepped back, made sure nobody was behind me, and cross drew my sword. I turned on my heels and walked.

"You know what to do!" Visada said to the group of senior officers monitoring the fight behind us.

Behind me followed Visada, Peto, a dozen Erskan, and two additional Treaslok warriors.

I reached the doorway that was supposed to be secure. Instead our forces were engaged in a sword battle with Loyalists.

Not missing a step, I waited a few seconds to find my opportunity. I brushed past two Treaslok and three Erskans until I was at the front and facing the Loyalists.

Swords danced around me.

My own blade sliced the air.

I cut through.

One Loyalist dead.

Two.

Three.

I took on two at the same time.

Cut one down.

Then the other.

I pressed on.

I hacked my way into them.

My shoulder was cut.

Not bad.

I charged in again.

Six killed.

Seven.

Eight.

Nine.

There was an empty hall before me.

Blood and flesh clung to my sword.

My arms were covered in blood.

My boots clicked along the hall.

I looked over my shoulder. The Erskans and Treaslok warriors maintained a short distance from me.

The bodies of Loyalists, hacked into pieces, lay scattered on the ground.

Then we reached a heavy set of locked double doors.

The Elite guard pushed her way past the warriors. "My Torino!" she exclaimed, clearly concerned that I had been fighting.

"Shoot this lock," I told her. I poked at the door with the tip of my crimson sword.

The Elite guard withdrew her StacGun and pressed the barrel near the keyhole.

She fired two rounds into the lock.

I made one kick at the doors and they flew open.

A series of stairs.

"Follow me," I said to anyone near.

Chapter Ten
Searching for Survivors – IV

"Stop!" I whispered to Mermak.

We held still.

I pressed my buttocks against the stone wall, trying to flatten myself.

"Someone is coming."

It was the sound of many pairs of boots, rapidly headed our way.

"They have sounded the alarm," Mermak told me.

I saw a door, twenty feet on our right. It was the closest option. But if it was locked we would be stuck out in the hall by the time the Treaslok go there.

"Come on!" I told Mermak.

We ran to the solitary door.

The sounds of the guards came closer.

I held my breath and then pushed on the door latch.

It opened.

Mermak pushed in behind me and   slammed the door shut.

The room was dark. We saw nothing and heard nothing.

Except for the sound of the guards' boots.

"Get on the other side of the door," I said.

We flanked the door.

I held my sword in my right hand, ready to swing.

The marching boots continued.

Then they reached our door.

And stopped.

I tightened the grip on my sword.

The door latch clicked.

Then the door was slowly pushed open by the tip of a sword.

I was ready to swing.

A torch was waved near the entrance.

The room was a simple and small cleaning closet, less than six-feet square. Mops and buckets hung on the wall. Bars of soap were stacked on a shelf.

The torch was withdrawn.

The door left open.

The boots continued past us.

I let out a big breath of air.

It was sixty degrees, and we were naked, but I still felt sweat dripping down my neck and shoulder.

"Netra," Mermak whispered.

We waited another few seconds.

I quick-peeked around the door just in time to see two Treaslok warriors head into the room that led to the dungeon checkpoint.

"Come on," I told Mermak.

Chapter Eleven
Searching for Survivors – V

We intercepted two more Loyalists.

They had only been temporary obstacles.

I cut them into pieces without a second thought.

My haste to the dungeon almost caused a tactical error.

Visada and the Elite guard both called my name as I prepared to walk beyond an unsecured door.

My impatience was getting the best of me.

I stepped aside while Peto pushed the door with her sword.

Visada waved a torch toward the room.

It was a storage closet.

We moved on.

We found a dead Loyalist. The yiminee had eaten her alive. She had probably blindly found her way down here from the main entrance above.

We continued until we finally reached a guard post.

I swung open the door, ready to strike anyone in my path.

The dungeon was unoccupied.

Ten cell doors lined one wall. Each door was wide-open.

"Torino," Peto said.

She had moved over to the right side of the dimly-lit room.

I came over to see.

Three dead Loyalists.

"Yiminee?" I asked.

Peto shone her torch over the bodies. "No, Torino. It looks like someone hit them."

Each had a ligature mark around their neck.

"My frey," I said. He must have heard the attack and seized the opportunity to escape. "He would head to the highest point," I told them.

Chapter Twelve
Searching for Survivors – VI

Mermak followed as we reached the ground floor.

Other than shouting in the distance it was otherwise quiet.

They were no doubt conducting a floor-by-floor, room-by-room search for us.

"We are going up," I told him. "We have to get a view of what is around us and then figure out how to get out. Maybe we can tie some sheets together or find rope and climb down."

He nodded, not entirely convinced of my plan.

I wasn't either.

We spied a nearby circular, small diameter staircase. I made a dash for it and ran up.

Mermak was close on my heels as we made many counter-clockwise turns.

Finally we came to a corner of a long, narrow banquet hall. There were several doors at one end of the hall, opposite and right from us. Our side, left, had two doors and this staircase. We had apparently come up the slave's service entry. Appropriate.

Light streamed in through a three-foot wide by ten-foot high stained glass window that represented a bird in flight. It was not the same bird the Erskans revered.

A dead Treaslok lay on a table to the right, farthest from us.

We approached cautiously and kept our eyes on the doors.

She was on her back. It looked as though others had tried to treat her wounds. The injuries were similar to that of the other Treaslok we had seen near the dungeon.

"Hmmm," I said. "Here, take her sword."

Mermak slid her sword out of the sheath at her hip.

Something caught my eye under the table.

I bent down.

"Netra!" I said under my breath.

Mermak leaned over.

"It is a yiminee," he said.

"Yes it is," I nodded. "Looks dead."

He pushed the tip of his sword at it.

"Yes."

"If I had shoes, or clothes for that matter, I would step on it," I told him.

He pressed the tip of the blade into the insect. It made a cracking noise.

"Armor plated, flying, and eating cockroaches," I said in English.

"What?"

"Children's nightmare," I explained, reverting back to Erskan. "This does not make sense."

Think! I told myself. "Mermak, follow me. This looks like a dinner area. There must be water and food up here."

We went to the other end of the hall and tried a door. Locked. The second door opened.

Mermak held his sword low to the ground.

"Is this the correct manner to hold it?" he asked.

"I have no idea," I admitted, holding my sword higher.

The forty-foot hallway was lit by two torches. Three doors were on the right side, the end of the hall had a larger door on the left.

"You check those, I'll go down to the end and check that one. Don't shout if you find food. Just come get me."

He nodded and went to the first door.

I passed him and walked to the end of the hall.

Mermak entered the room and disappeared from my sight.

I pressed the latch of the last door and peeked inside.

It was a moderate-sized room with its own window, though smaller and not ornate. It had crates on the right side, just in my view.

I pushed the door open the rest of the way and stepped in.

Ineer held the barrel of a Browning at my face.

"Drop it," she told me in English.

I let the sword fall to the ground. It made a loud clang as it bounced off the stone.

"Come in, Ranger," Corrigan told me in English.

I moved into the rest of the room.

Ineer stepped back, keeping the gun aimed at my head.

"Over there," she said, indicating the middle of the room.

I was so screwed.

"On your knees, hands on your head," Corrgan said.

I crouched down and brought my hands up.

Both of them wore thin gray chemical suits.

Corrigan stood next to five shelves. He sat a black metal crate on the floor.

"What are you going to do with those?" I asked.

Ineer laughed. She glanced at the open door and then back at me.

"You have a penchant for rearranging my plans, Ranger," Corrigan said, ignoring my question. He released the latches on the crate and withdrew a silver canister. "I have to confide in you, however, that I never counted on you providing me with a delivery mechanism for this."

"What?" I asked.

"The problem with distributing nerve gas across a large city, say, Antrana, is in finding a delivery system. But thanks to you, that's not a problem."

"Or in Dola," Ineer grinned.

I had no idea what he was talking about. Where is "Dola?"

"Conservatively," Corrigan said, setting the canister on the shelf, "we estimate half a million dead in Antrana alone."

"Where the hell did you get nerve gas?" I asked.

He laughed. "I'm a weapons procurement and sourcing manager. You figure it out."

Corrigan tugged at the zipper on his suit. Then he reached onto a top shelf and displayed a wicked looking gun that had a maroon tube on the top of the barrel.

"Know what this is?" he asked.

I shook my head.

"Chemical sprayer. Guaranteed to melt the flesh in a second. Think flame-thrower with an extra bonus."

"Quite messy," Ineer snickered. "Good for close-in confrontations."

Corrigan walked over a few feet to Ineer and handed the chemical gun to her. She pointed it at me and then gave the Browning to Corrigan.

Netra! I was going to be shot – and have my skin melted.

Instead, Ineer and Corrigan kissed each other quickly while he kept the Browning pointed to me.

"Be right back, love," she told him.

Ineer stepped out of the room.

"She's just going to take care of a little problem," he told me. "I'm going to take care of my problem."

I was pretty sure that there would be no way for me to reach him in time. The Browning would discharge twenty bullets in the time it would take for me to get my hands around his throat.

"You have wrecked an entire civilization," I told him.

"That is quite observant of you," he nodded. "I have more work to do here, though. Did you know there is more raw platinum here on this planet than in the entire Earth Alliance? Know where the largest mine is? Ten miles north of Antrana. They extract more platinum in a month than the rest of the Alliance finds in ten years. And the Erskans cast it aside!"

"You propped up your own government on the Treaslok side. Ineer is your 'front woman' because a man can't be in charge. You give them guns, they trade a little bit of platinum. You discover what the Erskans have and you coerce the Treaslok to invade."

"You could have been a historian," Corrigan smirked. "Except you won't be around to write any books."

Chapter Thirteen
Consequential Retribution – I

If there was one thing I knew about my frey, it was that he would adhere to basics.

Shelter or safety.

Food and water.

Then attack.

We found a staircase that zigzagged several floors.

Fighting had been intense on the first two floors.

I had lost two Erskans and a Treaslok until I moved from the back and engaged.

By the time we reached the top floor my blade had felled another six Loyalists.

Peto and I were practically competing against one another, though my body count was three above hers.

I slammed Loyalist number twenty-two against the wall.

Visada impaled the woman with a jab to her ribcage.

The dead woman slumped to the floor.

I turned left and saw a short hallway and moved toward the closest door.

The latch was loose; I pulled on the door and it swung open.

It was a lengthy canteen. Several gray and blue tapestries hung from the ceiling. Ten tables, benches, ran the length of the room, a pair at a time. The far end of the room had a colorful window depicting an *oriona* taking flight.

I stepped into the room.

A tall woman opened the door directly across from me, thirty feet distant.

She was from Earth.

She held an Earth firearm with a glowing red barrel.

Ineer raised the weapon toward me.

I reached for my StacGun.

Ineer would beat me to the trigger.

My breath sucked into my lips as I leveled the gun and tightened my finger on the trigger.

Three arrows whisked by my head.

Ineer dropped the gun and reeled back. Three arrows stuck in her chest.

She fell to her knees and clutched at one of the shafts. Her face became pale.

I ran to her and kicked the gun aside.

I was joined by Visada, Peto, two Treaslok and three Erskans.

Ineer put her left hand out to the stone floor to hold herself up. Her voice wheezed.

"You must be Ineer," I told her, in English. "Where is Alexi?"

She coughed blood to the floor and turned her head. "Fuck off."

Blood flew from her lips after I backhanded her with my left hand.

"Grab her," I said. "On that table over there."

Hands lifted her bleeding body. She was tossed roughly onto her back at the table closest to the stained glass window.

I leaned over her body.

"Where is Alexi?" I asked.

"I killed him," she said, trying to spit.

I pointed to her thigh. "Visada."

Visada strung an arrow, aimed at a distance of one foot, and let it fly.

"Hmmmgggh!" Ineer groaned. She arched her back in pain.

"She won't talk," Peto said.

I put my hands around her throat. "Where is my frey?"

Ineer glared at me.

I heard a single gunshot. It was nearby.

"Now he's dead," Ineer told me.

"Arl!" I screamed.

My hands grabbed onto her shoulders and I dragged her along the table to the window.

She struggled and attempted to hold the table with her right hand.

Visada's sword leapt out and came down on Ineer's right hand. All of the fingers were sliced off and dropped to the floor.

I roared and dug my hands into her clothes.

I lifted Ineer from the table and swiveled my body.

A trail of blood spewed from her severed fingers and she screamed.

She shrieked as I threw her into the glass window.

Her head and shoulders crashed through frst. Then Ineer's legs hit the side, which caused her body to tumble as she went down over the stone ledge.

Red, gray, and yellow glass shattered down toward me.

Visada grabbed my uniform and jerked me away from the window.

I waited a moment, and then moved over to the ledge.

Glass crunched at the foot of my boots.

Ineer lay sixty feet down, arms and legs sprawled on the stone.

The gunshot.

I turned around.

Peto and another Treasklok were already through the far-side door; two Erskans were headed in that direction.

I followed Visada.

It led to a short service hallway.

They flanked the door at the end of the hall.

No one moved as I approached.

They held still.

Peto's sword arm went limp. Then Peto took a step back as I reached the doorway.

I held my breath and moved past Peto.

Chapter Fourteen
Consequential Retribution – II

"Any last words, Ranger?" Corrigan asked.

"Don't use the nerve gas," I told him. "Just leave these people. You've done enough to them."

"Not even going to beg for your life?" he grinned.

"No."

"That's a shame," he said, raising the Browning to his cheek.

I clenched my teeth.

"I'll give you one more chance," he said, lowering the gun to his waist.

"No."

"Fine. And I like nerve gas. Very clean to –"

A flash of silver streaked by Corrigan.

Corrigan screamed.

The Browning clattered to the floor.

Corrigan's right arm was severed at the wrist.

He waved his arm in the air.

Blood sprayed from the cut artery.

Mermak stepped back, in awe; he practically dropped his bloodied sword.

I got to my feet and charged Corrigan.

Corrigan staggered backward. He placed the stump of his right arm into the palm of his left hand in a futile attempt to stop the bleeding.

I snapped the Browning off the floor.

I had to pry the remaining fingers off the pistol grip of the gun and let the hand fall to the stone floor.

Then I squeezed a handful of Corrigan's chem suit with my left hand.

I pulled him to his knees.

He whimpered.

"The only thing bad about it," I told him in English, "is that there's a whole lot of people that are going to be disappointed they didn't get to see this."

My right hand held the Browning. I pushed the barrel of the gun into his mouth and shoved it into his throat.

He gagged, tears flowing out of his eyes.

I felt the barrel press against his back teeth and I twisted the weapon to shove it farther.

He gurgled and spit blood from the corner of his lips.

"You are under arrest. And you're guilty."

His eyes opened wide.

I tapped the trigger once and blew the back of his skull onto the wall.

The shot echoed in the room; a spent casing fell with a "clink."

My left hand released him and his body fell to the floor.

I sat the Browning down.

"Are you okay?" I asked Mermak.

He had moved around behind me, away from the door. His hands shook. "He's dead?"

"Quite," I said. A expanding pool of blood formed around the corpse.

Pieces of flesh splattered the wall.

"Then… I am well," Mermak admitted. He tried to stand straight.

Two Treaslok warriors burst into the door, one with an arrow drawn.

I snatched the Browning and whipped the barrel toward them, my finger on the trigger.

"Alexi!" one of them shouted.

I hesitated.

They had Erskan ribbons on their blood-soaked arms.

I took my finger out of the trigger guard.

They did not advance.

I felt my heart beating. If I was wrong, Mermak and I were dead.

The Treaslok warrior lowered her bow.

I sucked a breath.

Tural came around the corner and stopped, sword in-hand.

It was the most beautiful thing that had ever happened to me.

The Browning slipped out of my grasp.

Visada appeared behind Tural and looked over her shoulder.

A tear rolled off my cheek.

Tural took a step. Then another step. Her face broke into a big smile.

She took another step and looked down at me.

I looked into her eyes. Then tears clouded my view.

She came down on me.

She pressed my body to the floor.

She wrapped her arms around me and squeezed.

Our lips melted into each other.

She was warm.

We held each other.

I buried my face into her hair and kissed her ear.

After a long minute or two she released her grip on me.

Tural got to her feet, pulled her blood-soaked skirt down on both sides, and pointed to her feet. "First, frey, you kiss my boots. Then, I take you home."

I kissed her boots. Actually, I "air kissed" her boots. They were covered in blood and God knows what else. I was not putting my lips on that.

Visada held her arms around Mermak. He had a steady flow of tears running down his face and buried the back of his head under her hair.

The first Treaslok warrior cut away the curtains at the window. She brought one over to Visada and the other to Tural.

Tural wrapped it around my body. "It will have to do," she said. She looked at Mermak. "How are you?"

He had a half-smile on his face. He swallowed and wiped tears from his face. "I am well now, thank you."

"Torino?" the Treaslok warrior asked.

Torino?

"Yes, Peto?" Tural replied. Tural crouched down and held me tightly again.

"Jurina Cinzia?" the one called Peto said.

Visada handed a radio to Tural. "Tural to Cinzia. Status?"

"Clean-up now. The reinforcements from the road have arrived."

"I have a gift for you," Tural said, smiling.

There was a pause.

Tural faced the radio toward Mermak. She nodded.

"Mistress!" Mermak shouted.

"Where are you?" Cinzia snapped.

"He is safe," Tural replied. "We will meet you in the courtyard in a few minutes."

"Thank you!" Cinzia replied. Her voice cracked.

Torino?

Tural had the siglet rank of the Torino on her uniform.

Was Sklera okay? What happened?

"You did that?" she asked me while looking at Corrigan's severed hand.

"No." I nodded my chin toward Mermak.

Mermak did not flinch. He looked straight at Tural.

Tural nodded. Then she laughed.

Tural pointed to Corrigan's body. "Visada, cut off his head – the rest of his head – and find a bag. It appears that Cinzia's slave will be presenting a very special gift to my sister tonight."

"Mistress," I said. "We need everything in this room taken back to the palace. And there are dangerous weapons here – extra guards would be a good idea."

An Erskan moved to stand by the door.

"Mistress? I'm not really up for taking a ride on a ship," I added. "The last one did not go well."

Tural laughed. She reached under my left arm and lifted me.

Peto, the Treaslok warrior, got on my right side and helped Tural carry me out of the room.

Mermak was assisted by Visada and an Erskan.

I looked over my shoulder at him.

I was serious. A ten-hour boat ride was not appealing.

He understood and shook his head.

Chapter Fifteen
Test of Will

The torn curtains were only slightly better than being naked.

The grounds of the courtyard were blackened by fire.

Erskan warriors were on mop-up detail and tossed Treaslok bodies – Treasloks that were not with the Erskans – over the side of a damaged section of wall.

Our small party was escorted by additional warriors until we reached one of several waiting wagons.

"Sit," Tural told me.

I hopped up on the side of a wagon. The doctor recognized me. "Frey? Playing in your barbed wire again?"

"He was rolling in it," Visada said.

Mermak sat on the other side of the wagon. The assistant doctor looked at him and shook her head.

"I never see any adult frey as often as you two," the assistant told us.

Both doctors withdrew clean damp cloths from the same box.

"There are several Treaslok warriors fighting with you?" I asked Tural.

One of them, Peto, pointed at Mermak.

I followed the opposite direction of her arm and saw Cinzia.

Cinzia used her arms to brush past a couple of Erskan warriors. She almost slipped when she rounded the wagon.

The assistant doctor barely had time to back away before Cinzia leapt onto the wagon and smothered Mermak.

I got a partial glimpse of his smile before he was buried in her hair.

"This will hurt," the doctor told me. She held the cloth near my right shoulder.

"That is fine," I said. I looked at Tural. She squeezed my left hand and watched Cinzia and Mermak hug.

"Are you cold?" Tural asked me.

"Yes, very, I think."

"I need to cleanse the wounds first," the doctor told us. "Then we will put warm blankets around them."

"Understood," Tural nodded. "Look at your legs! Those will leave permanent scars."

"Yes. I am trying to catch up with Jurina Cinzia."

Cinzia turned her head over her left shoulder and looked at me. "Keep going." Then she faced Mermak again.

"Ow," I said. "Ow. Ow. Ow!"

Tural tightened her grip on my hand. "Most of the Treaslok warriors in the city, Dola, were suppressed by Corrigan and Ineer. They are happy to be rid of them. The entire Treaslok economy was in shambles and the population is thrilled to be done with them. Not everyone is happy about Erskan control, but we are doing well. All of the Treaslok warriors on the borders have switched allegiance to the Torino."

I tapped the siglets on her uniform.

"Oh, yes. That would be *me*," she smiled.

I loved her smile.

"Torino Sklera?" I asked. "She is well?"

"Ah, yes. Everyone knows that she is my sister. We made an announcement and had a ceremony. You should have been with me."

The doctor was using her fourth cloth on my wounds.

"Did you find Ineer?" I asked. I should have asked earlier, but, frankly, I was quite tired and not feeling my best.

"I found her," Tural nodded.

Cinzia finally released Mermak and allowed the assistant doctor to begin treatment.

Mermak was naked and physically in horrible condition; but he sported a silly, euphoric grin.

"What did you do with her?" Cinzia asked Tural.

I noticed that Visada intercepted multiple command orders so that Tural and Cinzia could have time with us.

Peto pointed to the broken glass window, eight stories up.

"Oy!" Cinzia said.

"Here, wrap this around you," the doctor told me. A junior medic handed a thick tethan blanket to me.

Tural snatched it from her hands and wrapped it around my upper body.

I was not used to having this much attention and service directed to me.

The doctor cleaned the deep cuts on my thighs. Then she presented a shiny silver needle.

"Yes, please," I said.

"Alexi saved my life," Mermak said.

"You saved mine," I told him.

"When you were not in the dungeon, I was ..." Tural told me.

"We had a close call – the Treasloks were looking for us," I said, remembering the storage closet.

"That does not hurt?" Tural asked.

I watched the doctor tighten the first thread of the suture in my thigh.

"Mistress, it hurts like a mother fucker!" I told her, in English.

Visada was in the middle of a somewhat heated discussion with two senior officers. Tural and Cinzia caught part of the conversation.

"Please, Mistress, I will be okay now. Go," I said.

Tural kissed my forehead. Then she and Cinzia walked over to engage in the meeting.

"Are you okay?" I asked Mermak.

He looked down and smiled. "Yes."

"Done," the doctor said.

"Thank you," I replied. "I would really love to have water and something to eat."

Mermak nodded in agreement.

Six sutures on my right thigh. Five sutures on my left. I rubbed the threads on the right side.

The doctor slapped my hand. "Not clean!"

"Sorry."

She withdrew another clean cloth and wiped the sutures and my hand.

The assistant handed Mermak a flask of water and the Erskan equivalent of an apple. Then I received mine.

I slugged down the cold water.

Then I devoured the apple.

Tural and Cinzia returned. "Are they ready?" Tural asked the doctor.

"Yes, Torino."

For the first time I noticed that Cinzia's rank was that of a Korina Jurina. "Mermak," I said, "did you notice your Mistress' rank?"

"No, uh... Oh!" He flashed his silly grin again.

"Let us get you into another wagon, that one," Cinzia said. "We are going down the road to the foot of the mountain."

Warriors assisted us in loading to another wagon. We were able to stretch out under a pile of cozy blankets.

After a few minutes the caravan moved on.

I looked out the side of the wagon for a moment.

"Mermak, you don't want to know what the cliff looks like from here," I half laughed.

He snored.

I was beyond tired.

I just wanted to experience the stellar Erksan hot shower, have a bowl of wadu soup, and sleep for five days. But I was wide-eyed. It was that second wind. Or third.

Not until I was home in bed would I be able to crash.

The wagon ride down hill was fairly comfortable. It was a modern Erskan wagon – this I knew because it had steel leaf springs at the axles. Coiled springs were still several months away. Almost. And then we would construct shock absorbers.

About a half-hour later we came to a stop. The air was noticeably warmer.

"Next ride," Tural said at the rear of the wagon.

I pushed the blankets away.

Okay, so I did doze off.

"Mistress, I do not feel like I can ride on a horse."

She pulled my hand and helped me out of the wagon. I exited with one large blanket wrapped around me.

"No horse," she said.

Cinzia tugged on Mermak's feet.

I turned the corner of the wagon and faced forward.

I was still asleep.

Less than fifty feet ahead was a Holland-class ore hauler sitting on the grassy hill.

I rubbed my eyes.

It was still there.

Gigantic and looming, forty-feet in height, hundreds of feet wide.

The navigational strobes blinked. It was operational!

"Where did you find that?" I asked. "Did Corrigan have that?"

More to the point: how did they possibly know how to fly it here?

Sheri Jordan stepped out of the forward cockpit door.

"What?" I asked.

"She helped us," Tural said.

Jordan wore an Erskan warrior's uniform. She ran toward us.

Then she slowed down and stopped, about ten feet away.

I partially moved to the ground, so that I could kneel properly.

Tural clenched my hand and held me up.

Jordan hesitated and then moved another foot forward to me.

"Alexi!" she said.

"I…" I looked at Tural. "What? How?"

Jordan moved another foot and looked at me.

The air was suddenly cold again.

Then Jordan looked at Tural. "Oh, fuck it," she said in English. She reached her arms around me and hugged.

"Oh," was all I could say.

I put my left arm around her and squeezed, while Tural tightened her grip on my right hand.

This was really awkward.

Finally, Jordan let go of me and stepped back.

"So," she said. "You're a slave?"

Her words hung there for a few seconds.

"Yes," I nodded.

"Yes," Tural said.

"I am doing well here," I told Jordan.

"I can see that by looking at you," she told me.

I pulled the blanket closer around me. "This isn't my typical day, Jordan."

"Aren't you supposed to call me 'Mistress?'"

"I'm not sure," I admitted.

"Yes, he is," Tural interjected. "We will depart –" she paused and reworded her request, "May I suggest that we depart for Antrana and make continue this discussion in this presence of my sister? You need the Corona Compensator for this space wagon, yes?"

"Yes," Jordan replied.

"Then?" Tural asked.

"Yes," Jordan answered.

"Okay," I said in Erskan.

Uimisla came from another wagon and bounded towards me. "Alexi!"

"Mistress," I replied, smiling at her. I went to my knees and took her outstretched hand in mine and kissed it.

Then I stood and realized that Tural had not impeded my observance of protocol in this instance.

Uimisla gave me a hug and then stepped back. She looked at Jordan.

I don't know how women can do it, but Uimisla detected from Jordan that something bad had just happened and that Uimisla was now on Jordan's "B-List."

"Come," Tural said. She pulled my hand toward the ore hauler and we went past Jordan. Tural was not releasing her grasp on me.

Cinzia and Mermak followed – after Visada and Peto had a quick conversation.

The four of us reached the ore hauler's door before Jordan made a move toward the ship.

Jordan opened the cockpit door and I paused to allow Tural to enter. However, she gently moved me forward and steered me to the center seat. Cinzia maneuvered Mermak into the right seat.

We were allowed to sit down while they stood behind us and held the ceiling grab straps. This was a surprise.

Jordan entered, silently, and plopped down into the left seat.

She quickly cycled through the pre-launch list on the display.

I expected a rather quiet ride to Antrana.

But this was too eerie.

"How old is this thing?" I asked in English. It appeared to be older than the Tamagra.

"Registry is from '22," Jordan answered without looking up.

"How did you get it?"

Jordan paused and then tapped a panel switch. "Alberon," was her short reply.

"Thanks for rescuing me," I told her.

She turned to look at Tural. Then at me: "I don't think I'm fuckin' done with that part."

The ore hauler's low-power Corona drives rumbled and popped.

"It may be old," I said, "but it's nice to see a craft in working order."

"The compensator was hit," she explained.

"Ah."

"What about your ship?" she asked.

The ore hauler lifted from the ground.

"I don't know. It's probably fine. I never had a reason to dig around back there and inspect it. You can have it, of course. I don't need it."

Tural squeezed the blanket around my shoulders. "We must have talk of this later," she told us.

Jordan banked the craft to the left and we headed to the sea.

"Mistress? Did you find the northern Treaslok seaport?" I asked.

"It's ours now," Cinzia answered for Tural, in Erskan language.

I continued in Erskan: "Good. I suppose that the attack on the main seaport went well?"

Tural rubbed my neck. "It was perfect. Captain Stela made seeing eye glass pictures for you. We sank or burned forty-three ships and had zero casualties in the initial attack."

I looked up at her and smiled.

Her uniform was a mess. In fact, she had a fairly bad odor about her.

Jordan looked as though she was irritated.

"You used this to get into the fortress," I said in Erskan. "How did you surprise the Treaslok guards?"

"We dropped yiminee on them," Tural said

"I," Jordan said, recognizing the word. "I dropped the yiminee on them."

We rode in silence for another few minutes until we reached land. The sun was at our back and the mid-morning light illuminated the unbroken, wide grassy eastern plains.

In another moment we flew over neatly-partitioned farmland.

"Mermak. Food," I said and looked toward him.

He was asleep. Cinzia had crouched down to his side and held his right arm. She grinned at me.

"Where do I land?" Jordan asked.

It was a pretty big ship. I looked at Tural. She shrugged.

"Will it fit in the parade ground?" Cinzia wondered.

"I do not believe it will," I thought.

"We try," Tural suggested.

It was the first time I saw Antrana from the air. "Wow," I said aloud.

Cinzia got to her feet and looked forward through the clearsteel screen.

"How many people live here?" Jordan asked.

"About three million," I replied. "In the city "

"How big?"

"Around five-hundred square miles."

"No shit?"

"They've been working on this city for over two-thousand years," I told her.

"Alexi, guide her, please," Tural said.

"Yes, Mistress. Jordan, go northwest from here. There are five towers over there? Just around that you'll see the palace and the parade grounds on the southern edge."

Jordan maneuvered the craft over the parade ground.

Already several warriors and maintenance staff were in the process of moving equipment and bench seating.

I reached forward and flipped a monitor switch. "It will fit," I said.

Jordan gave me a "Don't touch my buttons" look.

She made the vertical descent.

A harfala of warriors rode to us from the inner perimeter wall. Sklera was in front, in full uniform, riding her horse a few feet ahead of her entourage.

We were almost on the ground.

"How did the Stars do?" I asked Jordan.

"What?" she asked.

She closed the final few feet and deactivated the engine.

I barely felt the ore hauler touch ground. It was a nice landing job.

"The Metroplex Stars?" I asked. "Did they win the cup?"

"Oh, dear fuckin' God," she glared at me. "Yes. They won in four games."

"I've waited about a year to know," I admitted.

She did not look happy.

I was not going to tell her that I was trying to get the Erskans to create a couple of hockey teams. One would, of course, be called the Stars of Antrana.

"Tural," Jordan asked.

"Yes, Sheri Jordan?" Tural answered as she unbuckled my seatbelts.

"What is your sister going to do with me?"

"We will have talk," Tural told her.

Jordan activated the control that opened the holding bays. Then I saw hundreds – no, maybe a couple of thousand Erskan warriors exit.

"I didn't know we had passengers..." I said aloud.

"Your Amazon friends wanted to take a ride," Jordan replied. Then she got to her feet. "Well, let's go talk to the head queen."

I tried to swing my feet over the side of the chair, but they did not move.

"Frey?" Tural asked.

"Numb," I said. "I'm not sure I can walk."

Cinzia opened the cockpit door and shouted out to one of the warriors.

"Here," Jordan said. She grabbed onto my left arm and lifted while Tural helped me on the right.

My toes were also numb and they barely felt the metal deck plating under my bare feet.

They assisted me out the door and into the sparkling sunlight. Then we moved down the three steps to the closely-cropped grass of the parade ground.

There was quite a hubbub of noise. Thousands of warriors moved about in orderly groups, talking and moving about. Overnight packs were slung over shoulders and crates of supplies were unloaded from the cargo holds onto wagons. Clearly, their ride on the alien space ship would be a story to tell for decades.

The women separated when Torino Sklera Kretahla approached and guided her horse toward us.

Three nearby medical assistants brought two patient stretchers.

Tural and Jordan eased me down onto one.

Tural pushed the blanket around my shoulders.

"Thank you, Sheri Jordan," Tural said.

Jordan nodded and faced Sklera.

Mermak, still mostly asleep, was put on a stretcher by Cinzia and another warrior.

A man ran up to Sklera's side and presented himself for dismount. She flung her boots over and down onto his exposed back. Then she dropped onto the ground.

Tural approached Sklera and made a smart salute.

Sklera returned it and smiled.

"You will not touch me, sister," Sklera said.

"Fresh from the battlefield," Tural explained. "Just forty minutes ago!"

"These are very fast," Sklera noted. She looked up at the ore hauler. "Can we keep it?"

Jordan stood with her hands on her hip, unaware of the topic of the Erskan conversation.

"Perhaps. Alexi can ride it," Tural told her.

Sklera's hands waved toward Jordan, "Then take the Earth woman prisoner to the dungeon."

I stared at Sklera.

"Oy, oy, oy," Sklera laughed. Then, in English, "We have fun at your expenses, Sheri Jordan. Alexi concerned we take of you prisoner and theft of space wagon."

Jordan relaxed her hands from her hips.

Sklera moved closer to Jordan. Jordan almost flinched, but Sklera opened her arms to a wide hug.

It was not possible, but my eyes stared even deeper into Sklera.

Jordan returned a short embrace, clearly uncomfortable.

"Come, we have talking now," Sklera said. She spun on her heel and mounted her horse with the support of the same frey. I saw a brand on his buttock that identified him as one of Sklera's personal frey.

Mermak and I were lifted and placed in a wagon. Cinzia dangled her feet over the edge of the wagon while she sat next to Mermak.

Jordan awkwardly stood on the back of a different male to make her way to mount a horse.

Tural quickly mounted before a frey could assist her.

Then our party moved toward the inner courtyards of the palace.

It would have been only a three-hundred yard walk, but it was beyond my capability. My legs became stiff; a cramp formed under my right foot arch, but there was nothing I could do about it.

Everyone had dismounted by the time our wagon stopped at one of the side entrances to the palace proper.

Sklera addressed the party in English, "All, retire for thirty minutes to clean. You and I shall go to the Council of Jurinas and await the others."

"My Torino," Cinzia asked. "My frey may be excused from the meeting?"

"Yes, fine. Alexi, I have see that you are..." Sklera broke from English and continued in Erskan, "are exhausted. However, I need you in the meeting."

I found my head tilted downward for a moment. I replied, in English, "A shower will help me, Torino, yes. Yes, I will attend."

"Thirty minutes," Sklera said. She waved her hands toward the door, "Lady Jordan, please come with me."

Cinzia and Tural waited until Sklera and Jordan went inside.

"I will see to it that he is sleeping, and then I will attend," Cinzia said. She motioned two medics to carry Mermak's stretcher inside.

"Follow me," Tural told my medics.

Fortunately we had only one flight of wide stairs to make. Being significantly heavier than the typical Erksan, though, the two female medics enlisted the aid of two males to carry my stretcher.

Finally they deposited me in Tural's permanent quarters. The two medics stepped out of the room.

Tural had the two males attend to her while she peeled off her blood-soaked uniform and assisted her into a soapy hot bath.

I watched the men rub her shoulders with soap for a moment. My face tensed.

Okay, yes, I was jealous. That was *my* job.

The medics returned and helped me to my feet. We walked out of the room and into the next quarters.

"How is this?" one of the medics asked when she pointed to the sutures on my right thigh.

"It hurts, Mistress," I admitted.

"I am concerned about immersing your body in a bath," the second medic told me. "We will wrap your thighs with these leaves to keep the threads dry. But it will be tight and may cause more pain."

"Understood," I nodded.

I could feel the warmth of the hot water while still a few feet away.

They wrapped my thighs with wide green leaves of the local equivalent of a banana.

They held my hands and let me ease down into the water.

"Oh, my," I whispered. "This feels so good."

The hot water came to my chest.

Literally, a hundred cuts on my body burned. My eyes watered when the medics lightly scrubbed the whip marks. The field-cleaning was only partially effective; this bath would remove the caked-on blood and dirt.

Then they ran shampoo in my hair and rinsed several times. My scalp tingled. I closed my eyes to let the water run over my face.

"Frey?"

I opened my eyes.

The bathtub was already drained.

The leaves were off my thighs.

I was completely dry.

One of the medics finished patting my hair with a towel.

"Frey?" the other asked again.

"Yes, Mistress, yes."

They had used Tural's asonga-scented soap on my body; the soft sensual aroma wafted to my nose.

"Are you prepared to stand?"

"I feel much better, thank you. Yes." I held my arms out.

My legs were stiff, but I was able to put my weight on my feet. I was handed a long palace skirt, and low boots.

It felt great to wear clothes again, even if it was not much clothes.

I was warm!

I tugged at the crude iron collar around my neck. "I need to get this off of me," I told them. "I want Tural's collar."

The lead medic laughed. "A lockmistress is required. It is likely that Torino Tural feels the same way as you."

Tural came into the room.

She wore a new dress uniform. Her rank siglets reflected the light from the oil lamps.

She was clean.

Powerful.

Beautiful.

"You look much better, frey," she smiled.

"Mistress always looks great," I told her.

She glanced at herself. "Now you can see me."

I slowly walked toward her and began to crouch down; but she reached toward my hair and pulled me.

"I know this is hard for you to move," she said. "You may kiss my hand."

I brought her right hand to my lips and applied a gentle kiss.

"Can you walk?" she asked.

"Yes."

The lead medic frowned.

"They will attend to you until we are in the Council," Tural said. "We must not be late."

Tural acquired two female aides and a Netratoh officer that I did not know. This was in addition to the two palace frey that followed us.

Tural received all sorts of attention as a Torino.

Again, I felt a pang of jealousy of others encroaching into my space.

It was a short walk to the Council of Jurinas.

Sklera sat in her throne, legs crossed before her. Her thigh-high front-laced leather boots extended through the slit in her skirt. Two of her personal frey sat on either side. Three female aides were also in attendance.

Jordan sat in a chair, pulled from the Korina's row, a few feet in front of Sklera. A palace frey was on her right side, slightly back, kneeling. He held a half-full glass of chusa juice for Jordan.

All of the males wore the same palace-style skirt and boots.

Korina Jurina Iona and Yannta sat at their places. Each of them had a frey.

Cinzia came in slightly behind us. An aide and a palace frey accompanied her.

"We will try to speak in English for to help Lady Jordan," Sklera told us. She pointed to an empty chair that was immediately to her left, up on the dais.

Tural moved toward it and sat down.

I was not sure where to go.

There was not enough room behind her because there was an old decorative wall that blocked the back; her right side would put me on the floor instead of the raised platform.

"Get a chair for him," Sklera pointed to a frey.

He stood and took the closest chair, from beside Iona, and brought it near Tural.

"There," Tural pointed to the lowered floor on her left.

The lead medic walked with me and took my arm to help me sit.

I might have been the first male to sit in a chair here.

"Thank you, Torino," I said.

"Is this to show me he is getting special treatment?" Jordan asked.

"No," Sklera said. "He is – how does Earth speaking say? He is all beat to hell. We care for our slaves and are kind for their health."

Jordan looked me in the eye. "Stockholm Syndrome."

"I don't have Stockholm Syndrome," I told her. "I've thought about that many times."

"What is this?" Tural asked.

"When the person's mind makes him care for people that have captured him," I said.

"This is good," Cinzia said. "It is normal."

I tried to find an example which they could relate: "In this situation, Mistress, it would be as if you were taken prisoner by a Treaslok and after ten days you wanted to help them."

"Here's the deal," Jordan said. She placed her hands on her hips and stood. "I must get back home in two days or they will send a rescue party. My destination was on-file. I need a part, a piece of the machine from the Tamagra, so that my ship will work. But first, I came here to take Alexi back with me. I am taking him back with me. Now."

Tural remained seated, but tapped her skirt with her fingers. "Alexi does not need a saving."

"Yes, I saw how he was doing just fine when I got here," Jordan told us.

"Alexi," Sklera looked at me. Her voice always commanded attention. Everyone listened.

"Yes, Torino?"

"Do you remember our speaking, almost a year ago?"

"Yes, Torino."

"Please speak of it to Lady Jordan."

"Jordan," I said. "Queen Sklera made an agreement with me that I could leave this place if help came. There are no strings attached to that."

"Well? Then say your goodbyes"

I looked at Tural.

I looked at Jordan.

I had a chance to go home.

Modern food. Air conditioning. Sports. I could home to Earth. Ranger Administration would give me a big parade. Interviews. Sports. I could have almost any assignment I wanted. I could get back to Tokyo. A promotion was a sure bet.

I looked at Tural again.

She bit the edge of her lip. Her fingers were still.

I would hate it.

"Jordan, I can't go back," I told her. "I owe you a great deal for saving me. You spent months looking for me. I can't ever repay you for that."

"Stockholm Syndrome," Jordan said. She shook her head and then huffed.

I stood to my feet and pointed at myself. "It's not Stockholm Syndrome." I looked around the room. "Jordan, how could I ever re-integrate with our people again?

And, why would I want to? I do things here than I can't do in Earth society."

"You don't miss home?" she asked.

"Sometimes, yes. I miss watching vids. And, believe it or not, I miss flying. But I can watch a thousand high-trained women warriors perform an absolutely flawless theatrical performance disguised as a fight simulation. And I can ride a horse at over seventy miles per hour across a desert. What I liked most about home was my job and helping people. I do that here. Every day. And bad guys? Hell, I caught one of those every week or two. Here, I helped an entire nation of four million people from an invasion – and I caught the bad guy."

Then I looked at Tural.

"And all of those things don't really matter as much as something else," I said. My voice cracked: "I love her. And I'm not leaving her."

I sat down.

"I am not leaving her."

Tural straightened her shoulders. She blinked a couple of times and then smiled at me.

"Fine," Jordan said, resignedly. She looked at Sklera. "Okay. Now what?"

"Lady Jordan," Tural intervened. "You want Alexi, your friend to be happy, yes?"

"Of course. I want his decision to be a good one. I do not like it. But I will try to accept it. I've spent a long time looking for him."

Sklera waved her hands at Jordan. "For your searching time, we can maybe make you happy good. Setala, here."

An aide and two frey stood. We watched them retrieve a three-foot by one-foot by one-foot metal-belted wood box. They sat it at Jordan's feet and opened the lid.

Sklera pulled her boots down and leaned forward. "You may have this platinum."

"Really?" Jordan asked. I knew she attempted to hide her enthusiasm.

"Only one string attached with this," Sklera said, using Earth slang. "You not tell others about Aervanta."

"That is all?" Jordan asked.

"Sorry?" Sklera asked.

"No, Lady Jordan," Tural replied. "You do not need to bring us ammunition."

Ah. I got it now. I looked at Cinzia. She looked at the ground, a bit sheepish. Cinzia must have pressed Jordan for ammo.

"I'll give you what I have. It's not much," Jordan said. "And I have two radios." She looked at me. "And a case of Mitey-Boostr as a wedding gift."

I laughed.

"What is this?" Sklera wondered.

"A drink, Torino," I replied.

"A 'wedding?'" Sklera continued.

"A ceremony to bind a man and woman together," I said.

Tural seized that immediately: "We have made a wedding on Twelfth Day of Jia."

Jordan looked at me for confirmation.

I nodded.

Well, it was sort-of a wedding.

"So, Mister Kretahla, congratulations," Jordan said, sarcastically.

"Are we done here?" I asked.

"I need the compensator," Jordan told me.

"Sure."

"How long will this make to happen?" Tural asked.

"Ten or twenty minutes," I replied.

"Torino, if I may?" Iona asked.

Sklera and Tural faced her.

"Lady Jordan. Before you leave us, you may help by loading and outloading our warriors from Treaslok?"

"Yes, of course."

Sklera stood to her feet. "We are agree?"

Jordan stood and moved up to Sklera. Jordan extended her hand.

Sklera looked at her outstretched arm.

I looked at Sklera and extended my arm and moved my hand as an example.

Sklera reached to Jordan and they shook hands.

"I agree, Queen Sklera," Jordan said.

Most of the attendees followed Sklera, Jordan, and Tural out to the east palace. A stone structure had been constructed over the Tamagra. We easily went past the guards and to the undamaged right-side cockpit.

Jordan surveyed the bottom right side of the ship.

"Fuck," Jordan said. "Oh my fuckin' God. You lived?"

"Roberts didn't," I said. "Oh, I've got some of his property to give back to you."

"Keep it," Jordan said. "It would raise too many questions if I gave it to his wife."

"I didn't know he was married." I waved my hand over the biometric control and the door slid open.

"Two months before you disappeared." Jordan looked over her shoulder at

Sklera. "I don't know how I'm going to look Dianne in the eyes on Monday."

"Oh," I said.

"It's not your problem," she told me. She brushed past my shoulder and turned to the rear.

"How is Burgess doing?"

Jordan crouched down by the rear engine release panel.

Sklera sat in one of the two dining table chairs while Tural hovered near me, listening.

"He retired in March," she replied, not looking back.

"There's a release lever on—" I told her.

"Got it. Here it is. It looks fine." She stood and showed the silver and red cylinder to me.

"Doesn't look too bad in here," she noted.

"It's been cleaned," I told her.

"Okay, help me with the old one, and then I'll go over to other side of the sea and get the troops. We can talk some more before I launch out of orbit."

We followed her outside.

We walked across the field to the heavily guarded ore hauler.

"Did you know there's a weird radiation emanating from the largest moon?" Jordan told me.

"No. What kind of radiation?"

"What is 'radiation?'" Tural asked.

Sklera leaned in closer to listen.

We reached the ore hauler and Jordan cycled the door control. "I have no idea what kind. The sensors didn't ID it."

"There's an epidemic of sorts here – either the males are sterile or the females are. The population ratio is about fifty women per every man."

She looked at me. "Well, what a guy's dream, huh? I bet you get sex all the time here."

"Actually…" I was saying.

"He is busy taking care of my needs," Tural intervened. "We will wait here while you make the fix."

Jordan scrunched her nose and then disappeared inside.

"Your friend," Tural said in Erskan, "has much acid in her voice."

"That is just her. She is – somewhat rough, Mistress."

"Alexi, this isn't fitting right!" Jordan said from inside the craft.

Tural nodded her head toward the door.

I pulled myself up and into the door.

"Sometimes it takes a hard pull to extract the old –"

Jordan was not standing near the engine panel. Instead, she pressed a button with her left hand and pointed a tube of drop-spray at my face.

"Wait," I said.

I raised my left hand out in an attempt to block the paralyzing aerosol.

Chapter Sixteen
Rescue from Aervanta

"Jordan, put it down!"

"I don't want to spray you," she said. "I want to talk to you, alone."

I kept both of my hands toward her. She was behind the rightmost chair and there was no chance of avoiding her shot.

"Okay, talk."

I heard tapping on the now-closed door.

"Lady Jordan?" came Sklera's voice over the ship's radio.

"You've been brainwashed," Jordan said.

"Didn't we just go over this?" I reminded her. "I do not want to go home."

"What kind of power do they hold over you, Alexi?"

"Listen, I've changed. I'm not the same person. Spending years in front of a psychiatrist is not going to make me feel better. You want to take me back to my old life, right? Think about it! Think! They would never allow me to be a cop again. So what's going to happen? You tell me. Really."

She paused.

"Tell me, Jordan. Officially, it's going to be 'Welcome back, Ranger.' And then after the media is done taking the vids, they'll ship me to Earth. I'll be there for years while they try to remove my experience here. You know the drugs they can give me. I might have the entire last year erased from my memory. And they could learn about this place and ...and then what happens? Do you think I'll be in the Police force for more than a year?"

The hand holding the spray wavered. "No."

"Then what do you want to take me back to?"

She held still.

"Lady Jordan?" Sklera asked over the radio.

"Alexi, I... I don't understand how you want to be a slave. You were a Ranger, goddamn it. Proud. Powerful. Now ... what are you?"

"Slaves here have a high value. All men do. And I am proud. Very proud. Don't you realize what risks the women here will take to protect a male? And it's not just me. They have made wars in the past to fight over a hundred men. There was one war, eighty years ago, that resulted in five-thousand casualties."

I pointed to the front viewscreen. "Powerful? I have more power now than I would ever have in the Earth Alliance. I am the slave of the second most powerful woman on this planet."

My hands brushed my skirt and then I tugged on my collar. "And, since you brought it up, yes, I am having sex. A lot of sex. I am Tural's sex slave. And I've had sex with more than a dozen women here."

"Yannow, they have a strong hold over you with that," she told me.

"It's one of several factors in my decision. Now, I really appreciate you coming to search for me. I appreciate you saving my life. But I don't need to be rescued from here. This is my home now. You may not understand why I want to stay here, but you do understand why I can't go back, right?

"Lady Jordan?" Sklera asked again. "Open the door."

Jordan put her hand down. With a long sigh, she turned to the control panel and pushed the spray tube under an instrument panel door. Then she sat in the left chair and activated the switch to open the side door.

Cinzia poked her head around the door, a StacGun held tightly in her right hand next to her thigh. She nodded.

Sklera stepped inside, followed by Tural.

Sonda and Iona stuck their heads and shoulders inside to watch. Then Sonda gingerly stepped in and felt the metal of the walls with her fingers.

Sklera moved toward Jordan. I expected her to unload an aggressive volley of words at Jordan. However, she looked at Jordan, sitting with her back to us, staring blankly at the front viewscreen.

"Thank you for not leaving with him," Sklera told Jordan. Then Sklera came up behind Jordan, reached over the seat, and gave her a quick hug.

Jordan turned her head. A tear ran off her right cheek. "It's okay. Yannow, I should be happy that he's alive. For the last year it was a pretty good bet that Alexi was dead. So..." her voice trailed off.

"The help of Lady Jordan is much liked. Lady Jordan is welcome to visit Aervanta again."

"We must look to the future," Tural added. She stepped beside Jordan. "I thank you, Lady Jordan, for saving my ... for saving Alexi."

Jordan chuckled. "Okay. Goddamn it. Let me fix this thing, and then I'll shuttle the other warriors over here. Where's the last place you want to be when I go?"

Tural did not understand the question.

I clarified: "Mistress, do you want to be in Antrana or Dola when Jordan leaves?"

"Dola."

"Okay." Jordan exited her chair with a slight groan. She took the Corona Compensator into her hand and then moved to the back center interior door and opened it.

"Hello, Lady Jordan," an Erskan warrior said in English.

The warrior was one of the Elite Guards, Sira was her name, I think. She, and two regular warriors stood in the buffer space between the engine tubes and the cargo holds. Sina cradled the Crest-Leeland heavy machine gun in her arms. An ammunition belt was draped over her right shoulder.

There was no question that the Crest-Leeland could easily rip a hole through the thin metal doorway.

"Alexi calls this an 'insurance policy,'" Tural told Jordan, referring to the stowaways.

Jordan let out a hearty laugh. She put her right hand on the wall frame and nodded to the Elite Guard, "Hello." Then Jordan walked out of the cockpit.

Tural glanced after Jordan before she turned to me. "Are you well?"

"Yes. She wanted to talk, alone."

"She might have asked us."

I shrugged. "Jordan likes to do things her own way. No matter how unreasonable it is. She might be Erskan."

I grinned at Tural and Sklera.

Cinzia lightly rapped the back of my head with her fingertips.

"Dola?" I asked. "We live there now?"

"Your owner has a nation to manage," Sklera told me. "There is much to accomplish."

"I have a special cage prepared for you," Tural grinned.

She recognized my frown. "But, of course, you can relax in my bed until you are well enough to beat."

I laughed. "I am very tired. I am looking forward to a long nap."

Jordan returned to the cockpit. "Done. Is anyone going with me now?"

Cinzia nodded. "Yes. Where do you want the platinum?"

"I will pick it up on my last trip. Let's go."

"About two hours?" I asked.

"About that much, frey," Jordan said with a smile.

We walked out of the craft and waved goodbye to Cinzia.

"I am very tired," I said to Tural, in case she did not hear me the first time.

She reached inside my skirt and pinched my right buttock. "Do not repeat yourself."

We watched the ore hauler lift a few feet from the ground, rotate about twenty degrees, and then quickly ascend into the blue sky.

Hundreds of warriors and frey continued to gaze after the craft until it receded into a dot-sized speck.

"I do miss flying," I admitted.

"Perhaps we could construct a space wagon in a few years," Tural said aloud.

I laughed. "We are very long way from doing that, Mistress. One hundred years, maybe two."

"Assist me with loading additional supplies for the next trip," Tural told an aide. "We should take advantage of the capacity of the space wagon and transport everything we will need for the foreseeable future."

I followed Sklera, Tural, Sonda, Iona, and other senior warriors to the palace and back into the Council of Jurinas.

Tural barked further commands to ensure a couple of tons of materiel would be ready in a half-hour. She also arranged for a much larger load of supplies be off-loaded from ships in Port Belenda and prepped for pick-up by the ore hauler.

My eyes blinked a few times and I realized that my right shoulder was pressed hard against a stone wall. Had I fallen asleep?

Tural placed her hand on my forehead. "Can you stay awake until Lady Jordan returns?"

"I can try."

Sklera and Iona joined our conversation.

"You should take him to a physician," Sklera told Tural.

"Yes," Tural replied. "As soon as we return to Dola."

Sklera looked at my legs, "Alexi, what happened to you and Mermak?"

I managed a smile. "We turned the Hios around when we saw a silhouette aft and starboard. It was a Treaslok warship. They did not see us until it was too late. We both crashed and each ship went down. Another Treaslok ship was following and stopped to pick up the survivors."

"The crew of the Hios?" Iona asked.

"A few of the crew could swim and were pulled aboard with Mermak and I. The captain of the ship recognized my description and kept us both; they executed the crew. I am sorry."

Sklera reached forward and gave me a hug. "I am sorry this happened to you."

I was quite surprised.

Then again, perhaps not.

I knew that the Erskans believed that protection of their frey was one of the paramount precepts in their society.

Perhaps Torino Sklera Kretahla, queen leader of the Erskan Empire, detected my hesitation in returning her embrace. She looked in my eyes and said, "It is not right for our frey to face such treatment in the hands of the enemy."

"It is what it is, Torino. I would take the same risks again to help my people. And, I thank you for allowing me to make the choice to stay or go. This is my home."

"Secera Tural," an aide said. "Please excuse me. Jurina Visada reports that the alien space wagon has departed Dola with forty-two harfala.

That was about three-thousand, four-hundred warriors.

"Understood. Copy the quartermistress in Belenda."

Cinzia crossed her arms and leaned in toward me, "Can you stay awake until we have returned to Dola?"

"I do not believe so, Mistress."

"Both of you," Sklera waved her hands toward Tural and Cinzia, "look like yesterday's sodo. Do you have a relief shift in Dola?"

"Yes, Torino," Tural replied.

A medical officer and two frey entered. The men carried a medical litter. The physician approached Iona until Iona pointed in my direction.

The frey set the litter on the floor.

"Relax, Alexi," Iona told me. She pointed at the litter.

I eased myself onto the litter and forced my head back. I did not want to miss anything, but my vision became blurred.

There was a persistent ring in my left ear.

I flexed my toes because there was little feeling in them.

"Review the manifest from Belenda and be sure we are moving the proper materiel," Cinzia told an officer.

I turned my head to the left, away from them.

"This might not be correct," was the reply.

"Yes, remove that. We need more of these, here."

Their conversation failed to hold my attention.

I looked at the mortar between two cleanly-cut gray stones. My finger reached out and caressed the slightly coarse surface.

* * * * *

"Alexi."

It was a woman's voice.

My hands pulled soft sheets to my chin and I rolled away from the noise.

"Alexi."

My eyelids struggled to open. I turned toward the voice.

It was bright. I shielded my eyes with a hand and looked.

Tural was crouched beside me, her right hand on my waist.

"Alexi, you need to wake for a few minutes. I know it is difficult."

I blinked and then looked at my surroundings.

There was a different wall nearby. Dark red tapestries hung from the intersection of the wall and ceiling, the tail almost brushing the floor. The lighting was brighter, made by several dozen candles, instead of the typical Erskan oil lamp.

The room was large, with several rectangular overhead skylights. Diffused sunlight was cast below.

I sat.

It was a sort of antechamber. Two massive doors were opened to an outside area. I saw several people walking by. "People," meaning, mostly women and an occasional man.

"Mistress," I managed to say. My mouth had a terrible brown taste.

Tural held a polished black stoneware cup to my lips. "Drink."

It was lukewarm wadu soup. It flowed past my tongue and warmed my core.

"Thank you, Mistress. Where are we?"

"We are in Dola, frey," she replied. Tural took the cup and handed it to a frey that I did not recognize. "That will be all, Juto."

"Yes, Torino," he replied with a nod before leaving us.

"Who is that?" I asked.

Tural laughed. "Oh? Jealous?"

I told her, "Hisu writes 'Jealousy in the heart of a warrior is the cure for sanity.'"

Tural smiled. "Ah, you have been listening while attending frey education."

I nodded.

"That is Juto, the frey of Monu. She is a Treaslok jurina and the current highest-ranking officer and representative. She was separated from her frey Juto on the orders of Corrigan and Ineer; they were reunited this morning."

"It seems I am missing alot. Much has happened in the last few days."

"You have been asleep for six hours," Tural told me.

Jordan was leaving! I faced the door. "Jordan?"

"She has made four trips across the sea. We are suspicious of an increase in the number of warriors on the Helaton and Jinjou borders. Lady Jordan took our warriors directly to the northern counties."

"Directly?" I asked. I feared the inevitable.

"Yes. Lady Jordan also made what she called a 'fly by' over the Helaton camps. We hope that will provide ample ntimidation to prevent the unsheathing of swords."

"Six hours," I repeated.

"Lady Jordan must depart. She is waiting for you to say farewell."

Tural took my hand and assisted me as I stood.

She held me steady as I pulled on lightweight black leather pants and a gray sleeveless shirt. My thighs ached as my heels pressed inside the low-rise boots.

I found my right finger pulling at the ugly iron collar.

"We will cut that off this evening," Tural told me.

"The Treaslok took your collar," I tcld her. "I could not stop them."

Tural pressed her hand against my right temple. "I suspect this bruise is related to that."

I nodded.

She kissed the sore place on my head.

"I have your collar," she told me.

"Yes? How did you find it?"

Tural shook her head. "No. I will tell you that story later tonight. Come."

We reached the doorway and I stepped out into the late afternoon sunlight of the Treaslok palace main courtyard.

On either side of the doorway, five rows deep each, lined a thousand or more Erskan and Treaslok warriors in full dress. The Erskans wore dark purple leathers and gold trim, sword hilts glinting over their shoulders; the Treaslok wore medium gray leather and silver trim. To my surprise they were also armed, with swords at the hip.

The warriors left a nine foot wide corridor ahead of us that stretched two hundred yards to the parked ore hauler.

Cinzia, Yannta, Visada, Uimisla, Monu, and Jordan stood at the door of the craft, facing each other. There was another unidentified high-ranking Treaslok warrior with them.

They turned to face Tural and I when one of several aides made a comment to them.

"What is the occasion, Mistress?" I asked.

I moved slightly behind her to take my proper position.

"The departure of Lady Jordan, of course."

"I guess she received a nice arrival also?"

"Of course."

I could not prevent the corner of my lips from making a frown.

We walked in silence until we joined the assembled group of women. All of them, except for Jordan, made an Erskan-style salute to Tural.

Her face serious, Tural returned the snap.

Jordan wore a Class Three flyer suit, drab, but perfectly comfortable for sitting in a space craft. My eyes were drawn to the glittering gold and platinum bracelet snapped around her right bicep. It carried the Torino's seal.

"Alexi," Tural said. She pointed to the ground.

I walked until I was at her side.

Tural reached toward Jordan and took her hands in her own and spoke in English: "Lady Jordan, we are grateful for your help the last two days. I hope that our small gift will please you and demonstrate our appreciation."

It was the most perfect English I ever heard from Tural. It was no doubt well-practiced.

"Yes, they are nice gifts. And..." Jordan looked at me for a few seconds. "And I know this is where he wants to be. I am good with that."

Tural released her grasp. Then Tural moved her head toward Jordan.

I stepped toward Jordan.

We hugged for a few seconds.

"I wish I could stay longer, Alexi. But I have to get out of here or they'll send a search and rescue crew."

"I know. That always helps when you have a chance to file a flight plan."

"I never found out what happened?" she asked.

"Corrigan, sneaky bastard that he was. He engaged a corona within a corona on another ship and broke out of trajectory as a decoy. We figured it out and chased him to Aervanta. Landed right in the middle of a few of their crafts. Best I can tell, they were about to unload a large supply of arms. I shot it down, but came under fire. I got them all, including Corrigan's craft. But we took a direct hit in the rear of the extended Tamagra."

"Yeah, I saw the Tamagra. Hard to believe anyone lived."

"Roberts piloted the thing down most of the way – even after having both of his legs crushed. It was a heroic effort. It's a shame we can't do anything to recognize that."

"Yeah. About that. I can't even take that fucker Corrigan's body back. Anything could raise suspicion."

"Nice bracelet," I pointed out.

"I have to get one souvenir. Oh, and I'm going to have a hell of a time finding a hiding spot for this goddamn nerve gas. There was enough of that stuff to wipe out a large city. A large Earth city."

"Speaking of souvenirs," I said. "Is there any –"

Jordan cut me off. "Your owner has a couple of boxes of gifts for you."

Tural nodded.

"There are items in there for several of your friends," Jordan continued. "You'll know which ones go to whom."

Uimisla had a stupid grin.

"Yes, even for the crazy engineer chick," Jordan grinned. "Look, man, I have to go. I wish we had more time to talk. Oh, one last thing. There's something fuckin' weird about the radiation on the second largest moon. I don't know if that's what is messing with the genetic imbalance here or whatever. There's an AMK Four in your 'care package.' Maybe you can re-tune the instruments in it to figure out what's bouncing around here."

"Thank you, Jordan. Thanks for everything."

She looked around my shoulder at the palace and then shook her head. "Just like a fairy tale."

Tural moved closer and reached around Jordan for a hug. "Shia-talso, Lady Jordan."

I stepped back a foot and waited while all of the women hugged Jordan and bade her good-bye.

"Alexi, brieneia," Tural said.

I hesitated for a half-second. Then I got to my knees and kissed each of Jordan's boots and waited. I could not anticipate what Jordan would say or do.

"Thank you," Jordan said. "I am honored."

I stood and took my place beside Tural.

"Tural," Jordan admitted. "I am truly envious."

"Sorry?" Tural asked.

I translated the word to Erskan.

Tural leaned into Jordan's ear and whispered.

They both laughed.

Jordan nodded and then swept all of us with her eyes. "Shia-talso," she said. Then she stepped into the cockpit door, waved at me, and shut it behind her.

Our group moved a few feet to distance ourselves from the ore hauler.

The clearsteel screen lightened and I could see Jordan with a bottle to her lips.

The engine popped as the Corona drive warmed.

Then she brought the craft a few inches from the ground.

Jordan made one more glance in my direction – we locked eyes for a moment.

I want to be here.

I know you do.

Then the ore hauler ascended to the eastern sky.

In twenty seconds it was gone from sight.

I barely heard the command to disperse the formation.

The craft was gone.

My only way home.

Except that this was home.

Now.

Cinzia put her arms around me. "Are you well, frey?"

My hand wiped away tears.

"Yes, Mistress. It is just the pain in my legs."

Tural faced me, "Yes, of course. You should retire to my room. Juto has been assigned to attend to your recovery."

"How is Mermak?" I asked. I had to talk about something. Anything to take my thoughts away from Jordan.

"He is here as well," Cinzia said. "He is resting. Thank you for your inquiry. And for saving his life."

"He was strong," I told them.

Cinzia put her arm around my shoulders. "I know what he tried to do. And I know you watched over him and led him to safety."

"It was very hard for him, Mistress Cinzia," I tried to explain. "They were –"

She put her fingers to my lips and pressed them closed. "I know."

"Alexi, come," Tural told me.

I followed her to the Treaslok palace. Once inside we navigated several wide halls and a rather large, circular staircase that was supported by marble-like columns. We passed a couple of Erskan Elite Guards and then entered a spacious room.

The room was appointed with lush flowers, colorful red, blue, and white tapestries, plush rugs of Erskan origin, and several oil lamps. Multiple high-backed chairs and knee-high tables provided seating for ten or more persons.

Three doorways led off from the main room.

I followed Tural to the center double-door which I opened for her.

Inside was a large bedroom. An Erskan steel-framed bed dominated the center of the room. Welded D-ring attachment points were strategically placed at different positions around the oversized bedding. In most places I would have called it a super-King sized bed, but here it would only be appropriate to call it a super-Queen bed.

Natural light came down to door entrance via a vertical stone shaft. Four narrow windows lined the south wall.

The other side of the wall held a steel cage that matched the twisted metal design of the bed. A sturdy pulley suspended a heavy eyebolt from the twenty-foot high ceiling.

I could see beyond another door and observed the restroom.

"Nice," I observed.

Tural placed her hands on her hips and turned to face me. "Yes. Welcome to my new home."

"Fit for a queen," I told her.

"Undress and get in bed. Juto will arrive shortly. Rest until tomorrow. You look tired."

"Yes, Mistress."

I stripped and placed my clothes on top of heavy wood dresser. I glanced in the platinum-backed mirror.

My legs did look terrible. In fact, I was in pretty bad shape all around. Several sutures. Plenty of bruises to make a pro hockey player feel inadequate, and more whip marks than could be counted.

It was certain that I would have permanent scars.

I might even catch up to Cinzia.

"Rest, my frey." Tural pulled the asonga-scented sheets around me. "Tomorrow we shall have that removed."

I pulled on the crude collar. "Yes, please. I will feel better after it is gone."

"Are you well?" she asked.

I looked into her eyes and knew what she meant. "Yes. I want to be here – with you."

"I am so very happy that you stayed." She leaned over me and planted a wet kiss on me.

Our lips melted.

I was asleep by the time she closed the door.

Chapter Seventeen
Gifts

The blacksmith frey dropped the slide-weight again.

"Ah," he said.

My neck tingled as the two pieces of steel fell apart and into his hands.

He straightened and presented the collar to Tural.

"Discard it," she said.

I pulled my head off the thin pillow and pushed away from the table.

"Thank you," I told him.

Tural pointed to the ground.

I swept my long skirt away from my ankle boots and went to my knees.

"You are mine, with or without the collar," she said.

She encircled my neck with her steel collar and fed the padlock through.

The single audible *click* of the lock was reassuring.

I let out a soft breath of air.

"Thank you, Mistress," I replied. "Thank you."

Tural kissed my forehead. Then she looked at Cinzia and Mermak. "Cinzia?"

Mermak's enthusiasm was apparent. He nearly knocked me from my position in his haste to hop on the bench and lay his head down.

Tural grinned.

Then she and Cinzia continued to fill in the blanks about the last few days.

"The Busai have been silent?" I asked.

"Kale is likely to plan an attack soon," Cinzia noted. "It is just a matter of where and when."

Tural signaled for me to stand.

I nodded at Tural. "I am quite pleased that the occupation is going well.

Destroying a military is the easy part; integrating an entire population is hard. At least in Earth history, that is."

"We have small problems, yes. These can be overcome. Their civilian population was desperate and ready for a change. An unexpected benefit was that the warriors most loyal to Corrigan and Ineer retreated to the mountain fortress. This left those that were moderates or anti-Corrigan behind."

"Another few minutes, frey Mermak," the blacksmith said. "Hold still."

"Cut him if necessary," Cinzia remarked.

Mermak twisted his head around to look at Cinzia.

The blacksmith put his left hand and pushed Mermak's head away from Cinzia. "Hold still."

"Have you performed an inventory of your gifts?" Cinzia asked me.

"He has not had the time," Tural replied before I could respond.

"I only ask because of the persistence of a certain engineer," Cinzia added.

Tural laughed. "Uimisla and her new toys."

"Ah," the blacksmith said. "One more cut."

The lock on the collar broke and the collar opened on its hinge. The blacksmith held the crude metal collar over a square pan.

Cinzia nodded.

He dropped the collar into the pan and pulled Mermak's arm up.

Mermak ran his hands around his neck. "I hate that collar," he told us.

I nodded.

Mermak went to his knees and presented to Cinzia.

She snapped her steel collar around his neck. "You are incomplete without me. You are my property."

"Yes, Mistress!" he half-cheered.

Tural nodded to the blacksmith and then she led us out of the ground-floor room. Several aides followed Tural.

It was somewhat unsettling. In the past, we walked alone, or with an Elite Guard. Now Tural spent most of her time attended by aides and senior officers. Cinzia was almost a shadow.

We crossed the east courtyard and entered the palace. I noticed Tural touch her abdomen with her right hand. She had done that a few times over the last two days.

Jurina Visada and Jurina Monu met us inside at the doorway to the recently-improvised chambers for the Torinos' Council.

Monu, formerly a Treaslok rijella, had been appointed as a jurina, a general officer in the Erskan military. Tural said it was an approach to integrate the military and provide Treaslok leadership. She planned to promote Monu again in a few months pending a performance evaluation.

A growing number of aides and Netratoh officers gathered in the front of the doorway.

When there were about fifteen women, Mermak and I. I looked at Tural. She was engaged in a conversation with Visada.

"Mistress?" I said.

"Yes?"

"We cannot enter until you do so."

"Yes, I know."

She continued talking to Visada.

Soon there were twenty women. Juto appeared and shuffled through the group until he was in position behind Monu.

"Attention!" Cinzia said.

The foyer area became quiet.

Everyone adjusted a space about five feet around Tural.

"My Torino," Cinzia offered.

Tural stepped forward a foot.

"It has been Erskan tradition that males are not allowed attendance in a Jurina Council meeting. However, we have made several departures from our traditions and now we make another. There will be the place for four males, the frey of council warriors."

Most of the women looked at one another, surprise on their faces.

"The attendance of frey is not a position of leadership; on the contrary it is to allow us to receive input where needed so that we may strengthen our knowledge and increase our power."

Tural waved her hand toward my area.

"Of course, my sisters, they will sit in the rear of the room. It is the duty of the freshman jurina to ensure the frey do not fall asleep."

There were a few discreet chuckles.

"And, I will provide the senior frey with a long pike – to ensure my jurinas do not fall asleep."

There was a ripple of laughter.

Tural faced the double doors.

Cinzia opened them and stood aside as Tural marched into the brightly lit chambers.

The décor was a reflection of the Erskan Council of Jurinas. There was a central dais, grandiose throne, four rows of tables in a half-arc with a split in the middle. Three single low-height chairs were in the rear of the room.

To the right of the throne was an Erskan flag colored in two stripes of blue, one of red, and one of white. On the same pole was a triangular-shaped pennant, half the size of the Erskan flag. It contained a slightly modified Treaslok flag, gray and white, with a silhouette in green of the Treaslok national bird.

Mono and Peto, the only two Treaslok warriors in the room, hesitated in their stride as they walked to their seats. They looked at the Treaslok flag, exchanged smiles, and then sat in the last row.

Peto wore the rank of an Erskan Netratoh officer and her seniority was grandmothered to being junior to Visada.

Everyone in the room waited until Tural took her seat.

It was a nice renovation job. The chamber was exceedingly well-done. Almost all decorations in the room were of Erskan origin, except a few banners.

Tural sat.

Mermak and Juto waited until the last woman sat. Then we took our seats and waited for Tural to speak.

I looked at the stone wall behind my seat.

It had an unusual diagonal cut pattern, with dotted lines that formed a pattern.

I reached my hand over my left shoulder and pressed my fingertips against it.

Cinzia stood next to Tural and handed her a few sheets of paper.

Mermak looked at me.

"What are you looking at?" he whispered, concerned that we would be noticed.

"Have you seen this before?" I asked.

He looked at the wall.

"What are you looking at?" he looked over my shoulder.

"Welcome," I heard Tural speak.

I nodded. "Yes, the wall. This pattern. I have seen this before."

"Perhaps in your Mistress's chambers," Mermak suggested, his hand cupped over his mouth.

Juto looked at us, his eyes indicating concern of his own.

I pressed my fingers against the stone again.

Where?

"I welcome Erskan warriors and Treaslok warriors alike. We have much work ahead of us to bring prosperity to these lands. Dola is on its way to being a city of wealth and pride among her women and frey. To ensure our objectives, I will fill half of the council positions within the coming two weeks. This will include the addition of two more Treaslok officers."

It was a sure bet that the Treaslok officers present were pleased that mass executions had been forsaken in exchange for integration.

"Have you been in the Erskan Council?" I asked Mermak. "Did you look at –"

Tural stopped talked.

"Alexi!" Cinzia nearly screamed.

Her voice echoed in the room.

I spun around on my chair and faced an entire room of not-too-thrilled warriors.

Cinzia had her hips planted on her hips. Her face was red.

Tural leaned forward, a bemused expression on her face. She sat on her throne, calf-high, laced boots crossed before her. She let her hand drop to the side, sheets of paper dangling.

Tural had the same kind of seated position that Sklera took when sitting in the Erskan throne.

My face felt warm as a big smile grew with the realization I knew the answer to the unspoken question.

I paused. Then I grinned at Tural and then at Cinzia.

"My apologies, Mistress Cinzia," I said. "You need to look at something here."

Cinzia hesitated and then looked at Tural.

Tural affirmed her trust in me by a single nod.

Cinzia stepped off the dais and walked between the rows of tables.

Warrior's eyes followed her approach to my position.

I tapped the wall with my finger.

She looked at the wall for a moment.

"To what am I looking?" she asked, a frown upon her face.

I tapped the wall again.

Her lips moved into a pencil-thin line.

Then she blinked and straightened her shoulders.

"By my heart," she whispered.

"Korina Cinzia?" Tural asked. She leaned forward on the throne.

Cinzia turned about. "My Torino. You... please," she stammered and pointed to the wall.

A couple of warriors stood to their feet as Tural made the brisk walk to our position.

Tural stopped and looked at the wall.

"What is on the...?" she froze in mid-sentence. "Netra!"

"My thoughts exactly, my Torino," I nodded. "Only I would not use that word in your Council."

"Monu," Tural said. "Approach."

Monu, as confused by the others about why a blank wall would hold any attention, quickly appeared at my side.

Tural touched the wall with both hands. "Tell me about this wall."

"This part of the palace is two-thousand years old. It is older than the great flood."

"Do you know the original quarry?"

"No, Torino. Why? What do you seek?"

Tural turned to face the council.

The realization finally hit Mermak. He touched the wall with his fingers.

"This," Tural said, and then paused. All eyes were fixated on her. "The material in this Treaslok wall is from a quarry mine thirty miles east of Antrana. Inside Antrana's Jurina's Council Chambers is a ten foot long piece of the original wall of the Erskan Council."

Tural turned to the wall and put her fingers on the etchings. Then she faced the women in the room. "It has exactly the same decorative pattern as this wall here."

There was a ripple of exclamations among the women.

"What?" Monu said.

I looked at her: "You and the Erskans may be from the same family."

Tural waited for the many conversations to die. She looked at me for a moment. Then she smirked at me.

Cinzia moved a few steps toward the front of the room.

Tural took the cue and strode past her to the dais. She sat in the throne and crossed her boots again.

"It is possible that we have a shared heritage. That is not too hard to believe. Though it is clear that the Erskans inherited the beauty and intelligence."

The Erskan women laughed.

Monu took the prodding in stride. She stood and addressed Tural, "My Torino. I have heard that Erskan ship-building technology is quite primitive. We would be pleased to show our lost sisters the art of *proper* ship construction and piloting – if we had any ships remaining to demonstrate to you, that is."

Peto laughed and clapped her hands.

Tural grinned and nodded.

Monu returned to her seat.

"Alexi," Tural said, "no more surprises for today."

"Yes, Mistress."

Tural looked at a sheet of paper. "Continuing to the next item: Border security. Netratoh Peto and Netratoh Colia will own the two major gates facing the Busai. I have permanently stationed a Crest-Leeland machine gun in a new camp central to both positions. A stone-paved road will be constructed between both gates to facilitate rapid deployment of the machine gun, several catapults, and mounted warriors. We can expect a full-scale attack since recent negotiations concluded on a sour taste."

There was another soft ripple of laughter among the warriors.

"Item Three, Reconstruction: Mistress Uim sla has completed her list of civilian staff to compliment the Civil Engineering Unit and has dispersed women to obtain a full assessment of pre- and post-liberation damage to infrastructure."

Interesting how the description changed from an "invasion" to "liberation."

"Item Four, Day of Mourning: In two days we will hold a joint esatolo, or day of mourning, for all casualties from last week. This will not include Ineer Loyalists killed at the mountain fortress."

Tural handed her papers to Cinzia before she added, "That is all for now. Korina Cinzia will issue orders for individual meetings later today. Ensure that that jurina liaison officer is aware of your location."

"Dismissed," Cinzia ordered.

Monu walked over to us while most of the warriors exited.

"Now, frey, I understand why the Torino risked her life to save you."

"Mistress? What did she do?"

"When she was given your collar by Kale of the Busai, she rode out and killed almost a dozen Busai on the battlefield. She is a woman of great courage and honor."

"She is, yes," I nodded.

Monu pointed to Juto, "Return this evening no later than twenty-six hundred."

"Yes, Mistress," he replied.

Monu exited the room, closely followed by Peto.

"Did you know about that?" I asked Mermak.

"No. I was unaware about how your collar was found. I assumed it was in the mountain palace."

"Ask Cinzia," I said. "I mean, ask her if you can find a nice way to ask her."

Mermak nodded.

I looked across the room. Tural continued to sit while Cinzia and two aides had a conversation. Tural touched her abdomen again.

She looked up from the papers.

Our eyes locked.

Her eyes sparkled.

Then she squinted.

I smiled and looked at Mermak.

"Something is different," I admitted. "Something is different about Tural."

"She does not appear to be ill," he said.

"Not ill," I told him. "I do not know what it s. Maybe she is holding a secret."

"Perhaps," Mermak suggested, "you can find a nice way to ask her."

Juto laughed.

"I am hungry." I stood and looked at both men, "Let us find out if we may be allowed to eat."

"We did not have much food in prison," Mermak told Juto. "But Alexi, he is always hungry."

I glanced at Tural and she caught my eye. She pointed to the ground at her feet.

Mermak and Juto followed me over to Tural and Cinzia.

"We will see what Lady Jordan has left with us," Tural told me.

"This way, Mistress," I said, indicating the double doors with my hand.

I guided them to a room which had become Uimisla's temporary work area. She was not present.

"Probably at lunch," I told Mermak after the women had gone inside.

He grinned. "Now I am hungry, too."

Juto nodded.

Three tables had been moved into the center of the room. They were pressed against one another to form a large work surface. Various gears of an unknown machine lay in carefully-placed rows. A hand-drawn schematic of a pump was depicted on a large sheet of paper.

To the right of the table were four SecureCrates, brushed steel bodies with sleek black hinges and carrying handles. The design allowed for stable stacking of up to six crates. Each was two-feet high, five feet long, and three feet wide.

"Juto?" I asked. Mermak was still weak and not able to lift much weight.

Juto helped me lift one SecureCrate to the table.

I pressed my thumb to the scanner on the middle of the crate. Juto lifted the lid which we put behind the box.

Everyone looked into the box.

"Wow," I said.

"What is that?" Tural asked.

I reached in and retrieved the notebook-sized device. "This must be Jordan's PIA, which in English means a 'personal information assistant.' It is a machine that has a great deal of information."

"You started without me!" Uimisla burst into the door. She held a small plate of berries and fruit which she quickly cast aside to a bookshelf.

"We have only opened one," Cinzia said. "Come here."

Uimisla joined the onlookers.

I activated the device and found that it was not locked. The flat screen display brightened and the menu appeared within a few seconds. "Nothing of great value. It would be nice if we had an encyclopedia – a large number of scrolls. But, ah, yes.

Here is what she wanted us to have!"

"What is this we see?" Tural asked.

A color, high-resolution map appeared in response to the prompts from my fingers. The top right of the screen filled with a blue, white, and brown digital image of Aervanta. The top left of the screen filled with coordinates, topographical data, and a control menu. The bottom half of the screen filled with a digital image of the surface as viewed at five-thousand feet.

"This is good," I admitted. "Jordan, eh, Lacy Jordan, made her space wagon go around your world. She used powerful seeing eye glasses on the space wagon. And this made map pictures for us."

"Map paintings of where?" Uimisla asked, wide eyed. She leaned over my shoulder and leered at the crystal-clear images.

"High level pictures of the major land masses…and, detail pictures of Antrana, the Renest and Brenada coastlines, Treaslok lands, the mountains to the north, and land to the east. The Busai are to the east, yes?"

Tural nodded.

I adjusted the coordinates and moved to our location. "Right here, is what Dola looks like from five-thousand feet."

The time-stamp was four days old.

"As a matter of fact, this is from the second day of the month at fifteen hundred hours."

"Can you show the painting of the sea port?" Cinzia asked. "The Sonoma was there."

I tapped the screen and moved my finger west to the coast. I zoomed in to two-hundred feet, found the warship, and focused on the pilot deck. I selected a female. The resolution was superb.

"Netra!" Cinzia said. "Captain Elos "

"I want to see the paintings of Busai lands " Cinzia told me.

My finger dragged the focus area to the east.

"Here is the closest city."

I had zoomed out to a few thousand feet and found an area with dirt and structures. But zooming in I found only the outlines of small wood buildings. Roads were covered with debris. I focused closer to the street-level range.

"Everything is destroyed," Mermak said.

The elation in the room faded.

I moved the display along the road. Every structure was burned to the ground. Burned wood and clothing flowed out of several buildings and blocked passage of the roads.

Juto stepped back a few feet and looked at the floor.

Tural turned toward him. "Who did this?"

"Ineer. Mistress Monu was not on that campaign. But others were. Ineer executed officers that did not participate."

"How many officers refused orders?" Cinzia asked.

"I have heard rumors that thirty officers were executed on the field for refusing to burn Ulo. Ulo is the closest Busai village."

"Thirty of their own officers..." Uimisla echoed.

Juto looked at Uimisla. "Thirty? Thirty is nothing. Ineer executed six resta in one day."

"How many warriors is a resta?" Tural asked.

"Two-hundred, Mistress Tural," he replied with a slow head shake.

"What was the size of the Treaslok military before Ineer and Corrigan?" Tural pressed?

"Fifty-thousand."

"How many did she execute?"

"My owner could answer that question, Mistress."

"She could, but she is not here now. You will answer my question."

He sighed. "She said that one-quarter were executed."

Cinzia gasped.

"Then the growth was from conscription," Tural thought.

"Yes, Torino."

"You said that Kale told you the Treaslok burned several cities, yes?" Cinzia asked.

Tural nodded.

Cinzia tapped the display screen image of the destroyed city. "It is no wonder they are angry."

I agreed with Cinzia.

"Turn it to the off," Tural said. "For now."

I deactivated the display.

"What else do we have?" Tural asked.

"Ah, this is an Advanced Medical Kit," I told them. I lifted the elongated console from the crate. "This is a good thing. You know that I have small medical tools, yes? This is much... much better than those. This can perform research. To explain, I can try to find out why there is a population problem."

"When will you have an answer?" Tural asked.

"Mistress, it could take several weeks or months of work. That is not a promise it will do so. We need to examine many people first."

"What do you mean by 'examine?'" Cinzia asked.

"It will take a small amount of blood."

Tural pushed her hand out to me. "Now."

"Well...understood," I said after a pause.

I pulled the protective cover away and withdrew a reusable sampling pad.

"Press any fingertip on that silver pin for a moment," I said.

Undaunted by alien technology, Tural pressed her hand forward.

There was an audible "click" as a needle stuck her fingertip. She did not flinch.

"Everyone," Tural ordered. She looked at her finger. There was a small dot of blood visible before she pointed it at my mouth.

I licked her finger clean.

"Press, Mistress," I asked Cinzia.

None of the women reacted to the sampling. Mermak cleaned Cinzia's finger; Juto took care of Uimisla. Each of the males took care of our own dab of blood.

With all the samples in the AMK, I looked into the storage crate and removed a small box. "This is replacement stock for this medical kit."

We put the crate on the floor and brought up the second.

"One StacGun. Five-hundred rounds of ammunition. And five bottles of a caffeine drink."

"What is that?" Uimisla asked.

"Mistress, it is something that you probably do not really need, but I think you would enjoy it." I put the drinks on the table. "We can all try this at the evening meal."

The next crate contained various items that Jordan had stripped from the craft. Two fire extinguishers, a stand-alone monitor, two self-powered outdoor lamps, and a box of top-quality tools.

I opened the toolbox. "Mistress Uimisla, you will very much enjoy this."

She looked at the glistening silver tools. She reached into the box and fondled a ratchet set. "Oh, yes."

I unfolded the printed manual and read the contents. "Looks like about two-hundred pieces."

She gently closed the toolbox and then yanked it out of the crate. "Oh, yes," she repeated as she set it on the floor.

"Two more radios," I said, observing the units. "These are not on the same frequency as the other radios, however. We can still use them."

We opened the final crate at its present position on the floor.

"What are those?" Tural asked.

There were nearly a dozen sealed packages of rations. "Food," I said. "Earth food."

"You may have all of this for yourself, if you desire," Tural said.

"Thank you, Mistress. I would like to share with you."

I reached into the crate and removed a blue-painted data crystal box. "This might be interesting," I told them.

The shielded data crystal storage case opened with an audible click when I pressed the release. The data crystal popped into the palm of my other hand. It was typical high-density storage, approximately a half-inch by quarter-inch by two-inches, clear except for a sliver of red on the base where the interface was.

"This is a ten terabyte crystal," I told them. "That means it can have many scrolls of information on it – but I'm not sure what Lady Jordan would have loaded onto it."

I held it before Uimisla. "Do you have the hand-held PZK here?"

She nodded, turned her back and opened a pack on her desk. She handed the silver device to me.

I jacked the crystal and watched the screen light.

"Holy shit," I muttered.

"What is wrong?" Tural asked.

"A technical manual. A complete technical manual on the ore hauler."

"This is good?" Tural asked.

"Happy good," Uimisla said.

Uimisla understood the ramifications of having the detailed schematics of a space craft. Not yet so that she could construct one, but because the diagrams would contain information about all of the components of the craft. For instance, my previous attempts to describe hydraulics had been only partly successful. I clicked through the index and found a diagram of the cargo door opening mechanisms. I held the small display to Uimisla.

"Happy good," I nodded. "This will be very useful to you."

"Hydraulics," she said under her breath. "Oh, yes."

She took the device from my hand and began to scroll through the color schematics.

This turned into a significant haul of presents for our engineer.

The AMK beeped.

I went over to the device and looked at the screen. "The first of the preliminary *data*, eh, information is ready."

Uimisla walked over to look while the others closely examined various packages of food.

I blinked at the display and managed to say "What?" before Uimisla spoke first:

"My Torino! You are pregnant!"

Tural calmly faced us. She rested a hand on her belly and nodded. "I understand. This explains why I feel unusual."

Cinzia put both of her hands on Tural's shoulders and then pulled her in for an embrace. "By my heart, this is wonderful!"

A wide smile appeared on Tural's face. "My sister shall hate me."

"As do I," Cinzia admitted.

Cinzia pointed to Juto, "Call an aide."

Juto nodded and slipped out of the room.

Tural and Cinzia released. They simultaneously faced in my direction and proceeded to stare.

"Uh," I said in response to their seemingly accusatory expression. "Probably, right?"

Cinzia asked, "Do you think I could be pregnant, also?"

"Have you often felt tired and weak? Does the morning meal smell unpleasant? Do you frequently have the urge to vomit?" Tural asked.

"No."

"Then you may not yet be pregnant."

"There is much to prepare!" Uimisla said. "This will be a joyous occasion. The Glow Ceremony will be amazing. A Torino is pregnant!"

A military aide entered, followed by Juto.

"My Torino?" the aide inquired.

Cinzia intercepted the young woman: "Bring a radio to us here. Have Doctor Elana meet us in the Jurina's Council in thirty minutes. I want four aides present as well, and the jurinas liaison officer."

"Understood." The aide ran out of the room to initiate the orders.

"Is the machine well knowing?" Juto asked.

"It is one hundred percent accurate," I told him. "Torino Tural Kretahla is definitely pregnant."

I looked at Tural and added, "With a female."

Tural smiled. "I would even be happy with a male."

"Several weeks pregnant," I added. "You were fighting while pregnant."

Our child. I am probably a father!

I wanted to push Cinzia out of my way and hold onto Tural. My face was warm.

"There shall be none of that now," Cinzia said.

"Erskan law is very strict on this," Uimisla advised. "It is all-encompassing and there are no exceptions."

"Correct, my Torino?" Cinzia stated.

Tural paused. She tapped her hip and avoided Cinzia by looking toward Uimisla.

"Correct?" Cinzia repeated.

"Yes, correct," Tural frowned. "No combat."

My hands opened and closed a few times.

"Alexi, here," Tural said. She pointed to her feet.

I darted to the floor and kissed her right boot.

"Thank you for your gift of life," she told me. She grabbed my hair and pulled me to her lips.

We kissed for a moment until she released her grasp.

A different young aide appeared with a Federal radio.

Tural took the device in hand and flashed a smile. "I will share the joyous information to my sister alone."

We exited the room as Tural called the Antrana Ops Centre.

Mermak and I waited against the wall, shoulders nearly touching, while Cinzia spoke to another aide that arrived. After a minute or two, Mermak rubbed his thighs, arched his back in a grimace, and then faced me with a hesitant look.

"Yes?" I asked.

"I hope that you can impregnate my Mistress, also," he confided.

That was a request I thought I'd never hear.

"Uh. I shall try my best," I finally replied.

"Mistress Cinzia would be much pleased."

Uimisla overheard our conversation. "Yes," she said. "You will be popular now. However – "

Tural's laughter poured out of the room into the hall.

"She is enjoying the radio call," Cinzia told us.

"Yes," Uimisla nodded. She grinned at me. She eyed me like a piece of meat in the typical aggressive Erskan manner. Though she was younger than most of the Erskan women I knew, and her ever-present child-in-a-candy-store disposition made her appear less-threatening, I frequently forgot that Uimisla was an Erskan warrior first and an engineer second. Which meant she could be uncompromisingly dominant, ruthlessly controlling, and sexually sadistic.

My feet shifted uncomfortably.

Thankfully, Tural peered into the hall. She handed the radio to an aide. "Oy, oy oy. The Primera Torino will personally attend the Glow Ceremony."

Tural tapped my chest with a finger. "And you, frey... you must quickly recover from your vacation with Corrigan and Inner."

"Mistress? May I look at the medical machine again?"

"Yes."

I squeezed past her and displayed the preliminary information on my test results.

"Ah, yes," I turned around to face the others. "I take a special medicine that prevents a pregnancy. I have to take it every two years. But it has worn off."

"What did you say?" Uimisla asked. "To *prevent* a pregnancy?"

"By my heart!" Cinzia shook her head.

I contemplated the scenario. "It may be that the Erskan female is fertile, but that the Erskan male is not. Of course, this is only one instance."

Uimisla reached to my legs and pulled my skirt aside. She examined my bruised and sutured legs.

"We shall give him another two weeks," Tural said.

I was pretty sure that meant being a breeder was the next task in my service to the Erskan Empire.

"Cinzia," Tural said. "You may not rog him for the next seven months."

Cinzia sighed. "Understood."

"Why not?" I asked. I probably sounded indignant, though that was not my intent.

"One of us must be available for combat," Cinzia dryly replied. "I am resigned to doing all the killing now."

Her voice was dejected and she looked to the floor.

The women and Juto laughed.

"Can you take twice the scars?" Tural laughed.

Cinzia was satisfied with her mock disappointment and chuckled. "Very well. To meet with Doctor Elana, yes?"

We followed Tural and Cinzia to the Council of Jurinas.

Juto and I fell back to the end of the group. He tapped my shoulder and whispered a warning: "By tonight they will have already drawn the numbers."

We walked past several guards and followed the women into the Council.

"What numbers?" I asked.

"If Erskan and Treaslok traditions are much the same, a breeding list is made once a male is found to be fertile."

"I already have sex several times a week," I said.

He stopped walking.

The women disappeared into the chambers. They would not be pleased that we delayed our entry.

"Juto, what?" I asked.

He shook his head. "You do not understand?"

"Understand what?"

"Several times a day," he said.

"For how long?" I asked.

"Weeks, months... until you cannot. There is a revered home in Dola where the male breeders live. They are fed the best food receive hand-baths several times per day, and live like a rijella."

"Oh," was all I could say.

Sex with different women several times a day?

Wow.

At first, it was a fantasy come true.

Sex with different *Erskan* women several times a day.

Then, a vision appeared of me in a body cast with a crushed pelvis.

"Have you known any breeders?"

"None personally," Juto said. He pulled my elbow toward the door.

An Erskan Elite Guard poked her head through the doorway.

"We are coming, Mistress," I told the guard.

Chapter Eighteen
The Glow Ceremony

I pulled the last suture from my skin and tossed it into a roughly hewn brown bag that substituted for a rubbish bin. Uimisla offered the AMK's remote unit to me.

"Thank you, Mistress," I said.

I pressed the remote against my thigh and followed the wound toward my knee.

"Such medicine," she said.

My legs tingled as the rough lines of the scar were smoothed and the internal wounds treated against infection.

I dropped the remote into its holder on the main AMK.

"It is not that I do not trust Doctor Elana," I explained. "I do not trust what Ineer and Corrigan may have added to the leather of the whip or to what little water they gave to Mermak and I."

"I can understand," Uimisla nodded. "If this shall hasten your recovery, it is happy good."

"We should treat Mermak in the same manner, Mistress."

"He shall be here shortly."

I paused and then looked at her. "May I ask you a question?"

"Yes, frey."

"How long will I be in the breeding place?"

Uimisla took my hand and helped me get off the table. She pulled herself onto the table and continued to hold my hand. "For most males this is a great and pleasurable time in their life. A fertile male may have hundreds of females mate with him in a year. The sex frey is pampered. Though you may not notice a great difference because of your situation as the Torino's personal frey. She will, of course, take on another frey while you are gone."

"Oh," I said. I had not thought about that. It was disturbing. I was under illusion that this was a monogamous relationship.

Or, well, not true, exactly. I had sex with a handful of other Erskan women. Tural, on the other hand, had only me as her frey.

Now that would change.

"Frey?" Uimisla asked after a moment longer.

"Mistress, it is – I have to become familiar with this. Mistress Tural has only been with me for sex since she collared me."

"That may be true, but it is not common. Frey, you would not want the Torino to be burdened by taking care of herself? You understand why she requires a personal frey? You know the service you take in care of her, yes?"

"Yes, that is true. I feel that it is my responsibility and duty to service my owner."

"You are correct, frey. Other frey must take your place while you are in breeding service."

"I have much work to do here," I protested.

"It may be that you share engineering time with breeding time." She smiled wryly and added, "or both."

"How do I find out what will happen?"

"The Mistress of Sa doh-La will carefully lay your schedule. This will be presented to your owner and to the Jurina responsible for Civil Affairs. That is a position that the Torino expects to fill with a Treaslok."

That might not be too bad. Most of the Treaslok were friendly to me; except the former naval officers.

The rumors of a shared heritage led to an awkward feeling of reunification among the Treaslok and influx of Erskan warriors and civilians. Neither side knew how to deal with it.

I grinned at Uimisla's subtle phrase about carefully laid plans. She frequently dotted her conversations with innuendo that became more apparent as I strengthened my understanding of the Erskan language.

"Netratoh Uimisla," Cinzia said, "is this frey squandering all of your time?"

I turned to see Cinzia standing in the doorway behind me. I did not know how long she had been there. She turned out and waved her finger.

Mermak appeared behind her. He peeked around her shoulder and smiled.

"Yes, come in please," Uimisla offered. She hopped off the table and pointed to it.

Mermak waited until Cinzia nodded her head. Then he briskly walked over to us and climbed on.

Uimisla handed the remote to me.

"Will this hurt?" Mermak asked.

"No," I replied. "You need to turn around so I can reach your back."

He lifted his legs and spun around.

"That is a pity," Cinzia grinned.

"We can hurt him later," Uimisla commented.

"This should make him well, so that we can," Cinzia nodded. She pinched the skin behind Mermak's right bicep.

"Arl," he squirmed.

The remote hummed as I treated the first of hundreds of partially-healed cuts.

After a couple of minutes Cinzia took Mermak's face in her hands, "What is wrong?"

I stopped the treatment and looked around at his face. His eyes were closed and his head bobbed slightly. He was peaceful.

His eyes popped open. "Nothing is wrong, Mistress. It makes me feel good."

"By my heart, I believed you almost to faint."

"Please, do not stop," he told me.

"That's something I do not hear often," I told them.

It took another five minutes to complete the treatment.

"Good?" I asked.

"Happy good," he said. "Thank you."

"Many of those scars will never face," I said. "But all of the inside flesh will be healed within a few hours."

Cinzia caressed Mermak's shoulder blades and ran her hand lower to his spine. "Such medicine."

I looked at Uimisla and smiled. She returned a grin.

She stepped back and pointed to the floor. Mermak hopped off the table. "You may thank Alexi for me."

Then, in a gesture I had not ever experienced, Mermak reached his arms around me and hugged.

Though we both wore Erskan semi-formal, ankle-length black side-slit skirts, our bare chests touched. I was not sure that I had ever hugged a half-dressed man before.

I was more surprised that I had a reaction than just accepting that this Erskan man was the closest I would ever have to being a brother.

At the hands of Ineer and Corrigan we had shared a terrible experience that tested the limits of endurance.

He was family now.

I returned the hug.

"On behalf of my mistress, thank you," Mermak said.

"She is very kind," I replied.

We released and Mermak moved to take position behind Cinzia.

She grinned, turned on her heels, and headed for the doorway.

"Frey, have you seen your owner?" she paused and turned.

"No, Mistress Cinzia. She has been running every place this afternoon. Meetings."

"She is trying to balance the work of the state with her personal excitement," Cinzia noted. "I know her well enough that this will be her behavior for many days."

"We will be best served by staying out of her way," Uimisla laughed.

"Indeed," Cinzia laughed. She waved at Uimisla and disappeared.

I nodded at Mermak before he trailed Cinzia.

"Your owner was devastated when she thought you were lost at sea," Uimisla told me. She placed the medical remote into its case and locked it into a sturdy metal-framed crate.

"It was not my idea," I half joked.

"I talked with Peto to identify Treaslok engineers for positions in the government. She told me that Tural and she were in a competition to kill the highest number of Treaslok defenders in the mountain fortress. At first they were tied at a dozen, but the closer Tural was to finding you the greater her focus and skills."

"How many did they kill?"

"Tural personally fell forty-three during that assault."

I blinked. "Oh my God."

"She killed ten or so of the Busai when she found out they threatened to take you and Mermak. She is the greatest swordswoman of our age. She was always one of the best; you have inspired her."

"Oh," was all I could say.

"Now you can understand, frey, why she is happy you have returned and why she is now pregnant."

"I kept thinking about her while I was in the fortress," I admitted. "I knew she would come for me eventually. We just had to last long enough."

"Mermak has told us about how you saved his life. Korina Cinzia is deeply appreciative also."

"I would do anything for her," I said.

"Yes, we know."

"Do you know how many women Tural has killed in battle?" I asked.

"Why do you ask?"

"It is a compliment but also uncomfortable knowing that she killed forty women because of me."

"There is an official record of all combat engagements. The last time I read the scrolls was prior to the invasion. Torino Tural was credited with over four-hundred direct kills. I would assume the number is four-hundred fifty, and a five- or six-thousand indirect."

This information did not make me feel much better.

"Come, frey. I want to return you to your owner so that I may begin reading the new information provided by Lady Jordan."

* * * * *

I cracked the shell of a nut and emptied the contents into my palm.

"Well?" Tural asked.

She sat cross-legged on a comfortable-looking wide chair with blue and gold upholstery. Buckles on her shiny-black knee-high boots sparkled. She leaned forward and placed both elbows on knees, an action that pushed her breasts against the supple black leather cross-strap top.

I stared at her breasts for a moment too long.

"Well?" she snapped.

I put my hand to my lips and poured the pieces of the nut into my mouth. It had a similar taste to an Earth walnut.

"It is good. Much like a nut from my home."

Tural nodded. "Very well. You will open one for me."

I used an improvised nut-cracker and broke the shell of a second Treaslok nut.

"They call it a kwiloberry," Tural told me.

"It is less a berry and more like a stone," I observed aloud.

Tural parted her lips. I reached up and dropped the nuts onto her tongue.

She crunched it in her mouth and cocked her head slightly. "It is not bad."

I could tell she licked her teeth. "Hmm. It gets stuck in my teeth."

"Part of the pain of enjoying the pleasure," I grinned.

"You will open another for me," she said after a moment. "These kwilo nuts do not grow in our climate."

"The mountain range on the north, and the sea to the left, make the weather much different than home," I observed. "The word in English is 'tropical.' I do not believe there is an Erskan word."

"What do the Treaslok call it?"

"I will need to ask, Mistress."

"Which 'home?'" she asked me.

"Pardon me, Mistress?" I asked.

"You referred to 'home' when you mentioned the comparison of the weather."

"Antrana, Mistress."

"'Home' is not Antrana," she said. "'Home'" is where my closest friends and frey are."

"Yes, Mistress."

"Before dusk I want to tour the surrounding streets. Fetch an aide for me; we are going outside."

Within minutes I followed Tural amidst a small entourage of watchful and heavily-armed Erskan Elite Guards. Two newly-acclimated Treaslok guards provided additional security. The different uniform types would be resolved in a month when the first of Erskan black or purple uniforms arrived for the absorbed Treaslok forces.

Jurina Monu walked astride Tural and guided her to favorite shops.

Juto walked slightly behind me. "For the last year these were the only businesses that were full of supplies   Ineer made the inner-city businesses give a false story that everything was fine with the world."

"It looks the same now?" I asked. "It has only been over a week."

"Flowers," he pointed to a line of flowerboxes at the windows of almost all of the shops. Each flowerbox displayed bright and colorful arrangements.

"They look nice," I said.

"Those are Erskan flowers," he said. "We had a prosperous industry of flowers, too. Ineer decided it was not beneficial so all of the fields to the northwest were plowed under to grow food. But the farmers revolted and fled to the mountains. She ordered warriors to stop them. It was a one-sided battle."

A Treaslok Elite Guard walked slightly to my left. She overheard Juto and added, "It was a massacre. Peasants armed with sticks and garden tools."

The warrior shook her head.

"The first military revolt happened after that," Juto said.

"Ineer agreed to step down from power," the warrior continued. "She 'surrendered' in the mountain palace. The arriving forces climbed the road until Ineer tossed boulders over the side and killed them. Surviving leaders of the revolt were taken to the top of the fortress and pushed over the wall to their death."

It was no wonder that the regular Treaslok forces found salvation in the Erskan invasion. Or, rather, the liberation.

"I am sorry to hear this," I told them.

"It is a pleasure to serve Torino Tural," the Treaslok warrior told me.

Treaslok civilians moved about the road. Everyone wore light-weight clothing. A few Treaslok military were interspersed through the crowds. A fraction of the population was male; they carried cloth bags weighted down with food and other items.

Occasionally a pair of Erskan warriors would cross our path.

The reaction of everyone that recognized Tural was, without exception, favorable at the least, and of celebrity "awe" at the most.

In addition to addressing her own interests in a change of scenery, Tural made a political showing among her people. Her people.

The Treaslok people often bowed. Most waved.

Tural returned the gesture, maintained a full smile, and often stopped to chat with people.

The Treaslok guard tapped my shoulder. "There was once a ukek at this time."

"'Ukek?'" I asked.

"A time period where no person is allowed outside," Juto tried to explain.

No curfew now. There were thousands of people on the street.

A broad smile came across my face.

I was not sure what to expect after the invasion.

Certainly not this.

Our entourage paused as Tural stopped to caress a few handblown drinking goblets. The shopkeeper and a female child rushed to intercept Tural. They both bowed and straightened the colorful smocks they wore.

"Torino, how may we be of service to you?"

Tural held a glass at eye level. The mid-day sun glittered and cast a sparkle upon her face. She turned slightly to her right side.

I knew the signal and covered the four-foot distance within a heartbeat.

Tural held the goblet out and sat it upon my open palm.

"The quality is superb. I will purchase one from you."

"Torino," the shopkeeper said, "there is no need to buy. I would be honored _"

Tural waved a finger a few inches from her own lips and interrupted the shopkeeper: "I will purchase one from you.'

The shopkeeper's face became flushed and she stammered, "Y-- yes, Torino. Two Dach."

Tural extended her palm again to me.

I fished two Treaslok Dach from my purse and carefully placed them in my owner's hand, both coins placed with the dominant side-up.

The woman took the coins from Tural without looking and bowed. "Thank you."

The little girl, likely her daughter, bowed. Then she bolted toward Tural and latched onto her leg.

Tural's hand quickly ceased the planned reaction of six heavily-armed warriors and my own half-inch of movement. I silently laughed at our instinctive movement.

"Sula!" the woman half-shrieked. She reached for girl's shoulders.

Sula's shoulders pressed against the tops of Tural's calf-high front-laced boots. Tural bent down and pulled the girl up by lifting under her arms.

Sula laughed and smiled.

"Hello, Sula. How old are you?"

"Five," was the proud reply. She accented it by twisting her body around and showing four fingers and a thumb to all of us.

"How old are you?" Sula asked.

Tural laughed, "That is a good question. Today, I feel like I am eighteen."

Was it safe for Tural to hold that weight? She was pregnant. Could it hurt our baby?

I bit my tongue. A few days ago she was engaged in more than a dozen bloody swordfights. Today, lifting fifty pounds was hardly worth time worrying.

"'Sula' is a pretty name," Tural said. She handed the girl back to the shopkeeper's waiting arms.

"Lonna, she is pretty," Sula told the woman.

Tural laughed. "Thank you. Bye, Sula."

Tural waved. Sula waved back.

I turned to follow Tural when Sula waved at me.

I paused. I was unsure how to respond to that.

"Well-meaning friendliness over likely-rudeness" was the protocol I learned several months ago.

I waved at Sula with my free hand before I resumed position behind Tural.

Tural stopped at more than twenty shops before we returned to the palace. It was an enjoyable three-hour excursion but all of us were relieved when Tural decided it was time to go.

We went past the two Elite Guards at the doorway and entered Tural's spacious quarters. I placed five of her purchases on shelves after repositioning a few of her favorite scrolls.

I lifted my English-Erskan hardbound dictionary into my hands and flipped to the back to the new section, "Erskan-Treaslok-English." I wrote "Hosana – Lonna – Mother" into the page with a pressurized pen I had purchased a few years ago from Amsterdam, Earth.

Tural's hands reached around my sides and closed on the skin under my arms. She had completely surprised me.

"Oy, oy, oy," she laughed.

I replaced the dictionary onto the shelf and tried to turn to face her.

"No, frey," she said. She held tight for a moment. "I will have a little Sula also."

"Mistress, I am very proud."

Tural let her hands drop.

I sensed her mood change.

"Mistress?" I asked. I turned about to face her.

"It is good you are proud," she said after a moment.

"What is wrong?"

Tural actually looked away from me for a moment. "This presents an unusual situation."

I resisted asking the question again. I waited.

"Do you remember that Erskan children never know their fathers?"

I closed my eyes. "Yes, I recall you said that once."

What did that mean?

Then the words rushed out, "Does that mean that I have to go away?"

"I do not know. An individual male has never been of so much importance so as to break tradition."

"The last time I checked," I boldly offered, "you were in charge around here."

"Yes. This presents a problem."

"What problem?" I added, "Mistress?"

"Treaslok culture allows recognition of the father to offspring."

"Oh?" I wondered.

"I have proclaimed that Treaslok culture will be assimilated to meet with Erskan culture."

I bit my lip while I tried to figure out where this line of thought was going. Then I understood: "You are worried about the impression it would make to discard a particular tradition to meet your personal situation."

Tural sighed. "Yes. That is the concern."

"Oh."

I looked at the floor.

"Permission to speak?" I asked.

"Yes, frey. That is what you have been doing, yes?"

"I may not be proper in what I say next, Mistress: I do not, at all, care for the situation where I gave up my other life on Earth to be with you. And then learn that I have to go away because I made you pregnant!"

Tural frowned. "You may talk freely, but raising your voice is not permitted."

She was correct. I had become loud in my complaint.

I took two deep breaths. "Yes, I am sorry, Mistress."

"There was no guarantee that you would be my frey for life. Is that what you believed?"

"Uh, yes."

"That is an error on your part," she proclaimed with a finger jabbed at my chest.

"But I am collared ... and branded to you!"

"I could sell you tomorrow if I desire."

"But..."

"You are property."

"Yes, but −"

"To be used as I desire and sold as I wish."

Her words stung more than any whip.

I swallowed.

"Were you unaware of those conditions?"

"I knew that, but − "

"And yet you made a decision to stay, knowing I could discard you at the drop of a feather?"

"Yes, I −"

"Why, Alexi?" she demanded, her own voice rising. "Knowing this, why would you assume to stay here on Aervanta?"

I realized my neck was tight. I stepped back a half-foot. She was going to send me away. I wouldn't even know my own daughter. Why did I stay?

"Why?" she shouted.

"Because I love you!" I told her. My cheek was wet with tears.

Tural relaxed.

My hands were clenched and trembled.

She moved forward and squeezed her arms around me. Her face pressed against my bare chest. "Then, my frey, we shall change the tradition."

A deep breath of air escaped past my teeth. I took another breath.

"Yes, Mistress. Thank you."

Why did she do that? Why put me through this?

"Are you well?" she asked.

"Yes, Mistress."

She laughed. Her right hand came up to my left nipple. She pressed and made a circle around my nipple with a sharp fingernail.

"Are you angry?" she asked.

"I do not understand why you had to do that to me."

"Do I need a reason?" she asked.

"No, Mistress."

She moved her head and lightly bit onto my right nipple. Then her right hand dropped to my skirt. She pressed the soft leather against my crotch.

"Tomorrow," she said, "you go to the breeder. In four days' time I will send for you to participate in my Glow Ceremony. I shall use the ceremony as an opportunity to indicate there will be a change in the Erskan tradition. Now, service me."

My cock was already stiff when I dropped to my knees and parted Tural's long skirt. I reached to her left side and unsnapped her cloth and leather thong and let it fall to the thick rug.

I pressed my lips over her and gave a single, teasing lick. Her hands took in my hair and pushed my mouth forward.

Tural's fingers moved to my collar and hooked the inside of the steel band. She pulled my neck hard against her. "Lick, frey, lick."

Long, upward strokes of my tongue drank heavily of my Mistress as her legs shuddered. She moaned and then lowered herself to the rug. She spread her glossy black boots while I kept my head between her legs and happily performed my duty.

* * * * *

My wrists were chained behind my back with a short one-foot line while the left side of my face pressed against the pillow.

Tural's right hand was wrapped around my waist. Her breasts pressed against my back and her belly pushed against the leather cuff on my left wrist.

I tried to blow the edge of the sheet away from my face.

Only a few candles remained lit in her bedroom. I watched shadows flicker about the wall before she snored once and kissed the middle of my shoulder.

Tural had several orgasms. Then she pushed me onto the floor and fucked me. She had pulled up and held my cock while I ejaculated into the air. She wiped off the spent semen and then chained me, tossed me in bed, and required me to please her orally again. That was several hours ago.

I was completely relaxed.

Another candle burned out and the subtle smell of the burned wick wafted toward us.

Tural's breathing was even and peaceful.

I heard a single bell ring out in the hall.

Tural's head shot up with a start.

"Mistress?" I asked.

"Alexi. There is a tradition of the Mistress of Sa doh-La that will run the usual course." She put her lips near my right ear and kissed. "Follow her instructions perfectly and you will be fine. I will call for you in four days."

"What?" I asked.

"Follow her instructions as you would mine. Do you understand?"

"Yes, Mistress."

I heard the single bell outside.

"Do not panic. This is normal. I tell you this only because you have not had time to hear the stories from other males and, to be sure, I do not want you to cause injury to the staff."

"What do you mean?"

"Do not resist." Tural unlocked the wrist chain and fed the chain out. I rolled over to face her.

"Resist, what?"

It was dim, but I could still read concern on her face. "I mean to say, resist, but only with delicate force."

There was a single knock on the door.

"And most of all, appear surprised," she told me. She kissed my lips and then pushed me from the bed.

There was another single knock on the door.

I pulled on my palace skirt and went to the front door.

Normally the Elite Guards would knock once the first time and then three knocks on the second attempt.

I pressed the latch and pulled the door inward.

Several women, clad head-to-foot in black leather, stormed into the room. Two of them went straight for my throat and grabbed onto my collar.

I retreated as one woman crouched down and snapped a black line around my ankles.

A third woman grabbed my left wrist and pulled me to the left.

I was sure I could yank her forward and step through the ankle line. The woman crouching over would go down with a kick. The woman on the left could be taken out with a single left-handed strike.

Tural ordered me not to resist.

I held still.

Then a woman elbowed me in the gut.

With a loud "hoof" sound I collapsed to the rug.

They were upon me with chain and locks.

In an instant my wrists were chained behind my back using the already-worn leather cuffs. My ankles were chained and a heavy leather hood tossed over my head. It was belted snugly about my neck, over the steel collar.

The women's boots shuffled on the rug and their leather outfits squeaked while they finished placing me in bondage.

With my head at ground-level I detected the soft sound of Tural's bare feet cross the stone floor. I knew her sound.

"On your feet, frey!" an unknown female ordered. She accented her command by jerking on my right elbow.

I rolled to my right side and groared while I attempted to stand without the use of my hands.

Once on my feet they connected a lead to the oversized collar.

I feigned pulling away from it until two hands grabbed my shoulders and pushed me forward.

My skirt was unbelted and I was stripped raked.

"Walk!"

The lead was pulled.

I had no choice but to do as instructed.

It was a good thing I wore a hood because they probably would have been less than impressed with my smile.

I was escorted on a brisk walk. My sense of direction was not yet established in the Treaslok palace; I was unsure where they took me.

We descended the palace by only a few flights of circular stairs. I was fairly certain that we stopped at mid-height of the palace. This was a good sign because the lower levels were undoubtedly the more uncomfortable dungeon- or dungeon-like areas. Typically, the higher the floor the better the room quality.

One of the guards rang a single bell when we stepped out of the staircase. Then they made me walk on a straight hallway. The bell rang again when we stopped.

I heard a door open.

Another bell ring.

A tug on the lead and I walked inside.

Questions came to me. Would they put me in a bed for this? Or was there a special recliner?

Would I stand in a window under a red light, flashing my legs in an attempt to find customers?

I nearly laughed out loud at that last thought. Of all possible scenarios, that was the most unlikely.

Still. How many Dach could I make in four days?

Two bells.

"Kneel before me," a gravel-voiced woman ordered in Erskan language.

The chains between my wrists rattled as I effortlessly went to my knees.

"You are Alexi, property of Tural, House Kretahla."

It was not a question. To be safe, I nodded.

"I am Deasa, Mistress of the Sa doh-La. Your ownership has been transferred. You are now my property. Do you understand?"

"Understood, Mistress Deasa."

"Spread your knees, frey."

I moved my ankles farther apart.

"Spread your knees," she said, her voice louder.

I strained to widen my stance without falling forward. Tendons in my thighs protested.

"This is your schedule for today. Cleaning, morning meal, rest, cleaning, service, cleaning, service, cleaning, mid-day meal, rest, cleaning, service, rest, cleaning, service, cleaning, evening meal, rest, cleaning, service, rest, cleaning, service, cleaning, retire."

I completely lost track of what she said.

"Do you understand?"

"No, Mistress. That was too much."

I barely heard the sound of leather sailing in the air before I was stung on my top right shoulder blade.

"Uh," came the involuntary voice of pain from my mouth.

"I shall repeat. Cleaning, morning meal, rest, cleaning, service, cleaning, service, cleaning, mid-day meal, rest, cleaning, service, rest, cleaning, service, cleaning, evening meal, rest, cleaning, service, rest, cleaning, service, cleaning, retire."

I tried to focus on the 'service' part, which was twice between the meals.

"Do you understand?"

"Cleaning, meal, rest, cleaning, service, cleaning, service, cleaning, meal, rest..." I paused. "cleaning, service, cleaning – no, rest, then cleaning, service, cleaning, meal. Ah, then rest, cleaning, service, and rest, cleaning, service, cleaning. And sleep."

"Almost correct."

A whip hit my other shoulder blade. It was at half the force of the previous strike.

"Do you have questions, frey?"

"Yes, Mistress."

"I do not want to hear them," she replied. "Take him."

Hands reached inside my elbows and pulled me to my feet. This was good because my thighs were almost useless from being stretched apart.

The bell rang three times.

Then I was escorted about sixty feet to a point where a door was opened and shut behind us.

"Kneel," the woman on my right told me.

I went to my knees and waited.

The hood was pulled from my head.

The room was brightly lit with a combination of Erskan oil lamps and Treaslok candles. It was a bathroom. Four large brass bathtubs were evenly spaced on the white marbled floor. Red and black tapestries hung from the ceiling and obscured the rough stone walls. Each corner of the room was decorated with a waist-high pedestal that was covered with an Erskan vine. The décor was what I would call Romanesque, circa 50 B.C.

The two women guards were dressed in a style I had not previously seen. They had discarded the black leather and wore Erskan-red, long flowing skirts, slit on both sides and trimmed in thin gold cloth. A gold belt was slung low on their curvaceous hips; it was made of interlocking metal squares. They wore neatly-pressed white pullover sleeveless tops with a plunging neckline and straight, high collar. It was "strict school teacher meets Roman goddess."

Gold spiral bracelets were worn on each bicep. The decorative insignia was unknown to me.

Each carried a red whip coiled at the belt along with a length of chain and two gold locks.

"Virsa," the woman on the right pointed at herself. "Corala," she pointed at the other woman.

Virsa appeared to be in her mid-twenties; Corala was a few years younger.

Corala moved behind me and unlocked the chain from my wrist cuffs.

Virsa reached to a valve on the closest brass tub and began a flow of hot water.

Corala removed the leather cuffs and placed the restraints on a nearby table. I waited for instructions.

The tub was approximately half-full when the Virsa poured a small cup of liquid into the stream. Then she snapped her fingers and pointed.

I hopped to my feet and walked to the side.

Corala actually held my hand to steady my entrance into the hot water.

I eased into the hot water and paused when I reached my crotch. They would have nothing of a delay; both women gently pushed my shoulders down until I sat in the tub. The water came up to my chest.

I looked for the soap. Erskan women used a round, gentle-shaped bar of soap; Erksan men used a rectangular bar. My visual search was unsuccessful.

Corala reached to a table and returned with two round bars of soap. She took a sniff of them and handed one across the tub.

"Arms out," Virsa ordered.

I blinked. I was paralyzed by the unbelievably nice treatment.

Words formed on her lips but I instantly complied before she spoke.

They took my hands, dipped the soap into the water of the tub, and proceeded to lather my arms from fingertip to shoulder.

Pampered? Did Juto say that the breeding males were pampered?

Each woman produced a small brass flask of water and rinsed my arms. I retracted my hands to put them away when both women slapped my wrists.

"Remain still until I order differently," Virsa instructed me.

"Understood, Mistress."

My triceps became sore and my hands wavered while the women put the soap aside and poured liquid into their hands.

"Eyes closed," Virsa said.

I closed my eyes. They poured warm water over my head and rubbed the shampoo into my scalp.

My fingers were numb and both shoulders protested.

It was typical Erskan: royal treatment with simultaneous suffering.

To my disdain, they finished rinsing the shampoo and then repeated the process.

"Hold your hands up!" Virsa, on my right, ordered.

Through clenched teeth I replied, "Yes, Mistress."

Warm water poured down my face.

They gently rubbed my face with a soapy cloth and then cleaned my ears.

Warm water rinse.

Dry towel on the face.

My arms screamed.

"Eyes open, hands down," Virsa ordered.

"Thank you, Mistress," I offered. I almost failed in my effort to guide my hands to a soft landing in the water. Splashing Erskan women would not be a good technique to win kindness.

Wide-eyed, I watched as Virsa and Corala soaped my chest, arms, and torso. As expected, they had no hesitation to washing my genitals. They washed my legs and then changed positions.

Virsa rolled a small table to the tub and took my right hand. Corala raised my feet out of the water and positioned them on a padded, floating block of wood.

It was my first ever combination pedicure and manicure.

And I enjoyed it.

I wanted to tell Virsa and Corala how nice that was. But the only words I knew could be said in this situation were "Thank you, Mistress."

Virsa nodded her reply as she completed my left hand.

Corala pushed my feet into the tub and removed the float. The women stood on either side and waited for me to stand. I got to my feet and was assisted by Virsa to exit.

Two other women entered the room. Both glanced at me for a moment and then proceeded to fill another tub with water.

Corala came around the tub holding a large towel. She wrapped it around my body and pressed until I was dry.

"Follow," Virsa told me. Naked, I followed her into another room. Corala trailed until we came into a small room with two simple beds raised about three feet off the floor. "On," Virsa instructed.

I hopped up. Corala pushed my shoulder down so I was flat on the starched, white narrow sheets.

My wrists were cuffed and chained flat above my head; ankles were stretched slightly apart when they were restrained in a similar manner.

Virsa appeared at the foot of the bed with a glistening-sharp shaving blade.

My toes involuntarily twitched and my arm muscles contracted.

"You are shaved clean, but not close enough," Virsa stated.

Tural required that I self-shaved my pubic hair. It was always difficult for me; this would be a different kind of "difficult."

"Still," Corala said. It was the first time she had given an order.

"If you want to keep these," Virsa said as she pulled on my scrotum, "you will be motionless."

"Yes, Mistress," I said.

She flicked the blade with her thumb.

They needed more candle-light. There were less than fifty candles in the room. They should have had twice that many to do this!

Corala placed her right hand on my abdomen and moved it toward my feet until she curved her fingers around the base of my penis. Then she pressed firmly to hold me still.

Virsa produced a white cloth and wiped her blade. She leaned over my thigh and pinched my scrotum.

I wanted to talk. To tell her – plead - "please be careful!"

"Breath, frey," Corala said.

I held my breath.

Virsa slid the blade.

I exhaled.

Virsa held the blade in the air, "No blood."

"Thus far," Corala shrugged.

The second shaving stroke was also okay.

Virsa quickened her pace.

"The frey is pale," Corala said.

Don't look away at me! Watch what you are doing!

Virsa continued her work.

Corala continued to hold my lower torso still.

Virsa raised the blade, wiped it clean, and put both in a white, thin wood basket.

Corala released her grasp and proceeded to wipe my crotch area with a slightly damp cloth.

They released the restraints and I slid off the table.

"Follow," Virsa instructed.

I was led into a long hallway that had twenty doors on either side, each relatively close to one another. The doors were of a medium-grade wood, had a head-high metal sliding peephole with locking hasp.

"Sixteen is yours," Virsa told me.

We stopped at a door Number Sixteen.

Corala opened the door.

It was a small room that contained a low table, low stool, and several candles. Scrambled eggs, Erskan-style, bacon-like meat, wera-fruit juice, and bread were on the table.

"Twenty minutes to eat," Virsa said.

I entered the room.

They closed and locked the door.

I quickly ate breakfast and waited for the door to open.

This experience was much different than my first one of being captive by Erskans. My guards were only strict in the typical Erskan manner; they were not aggressive and instead maintained a mostly impersonal demeanor. Not abusive, but they definitely possessed the female inclination to assert their dominance over a male. Which was usually demonstrated by creative torment whenever the opportunity arose.

I rubbed my triceps for a moment and flexed my shoulders.

At least they did not instruct me to hold something heavy in my hands.

Virsa and Corala appeared in what was probably exactly twenty minutes.

I stood and followed them into the hallway. Two other similarly-dressed guards stood three doors down. One nodded toward us and Virsa nodded in return.

Virsa directed me to another hallway of rooms, the doors spread out much farther apart. I went to door Number Sixteen. The door we had come through was closed behind us. It was a heavy wood door with metal reinforcement straps.

The door at the other end of the hallways was painted in an Erskan blue and appeared to lightly constructed only of wood.

"You rest for one hour," Virsa told me. She unlocked the door and pulled it open.

"Yes, Mistress," I said. I walked halfway in and turned about.

"My I ask Mistress a question? So that I may be better prepared."

Virsa's fingers tightened on the door latch. She paused, "Frey. You may ask."

"After one hour, then what?"

Virsa frowned. It was a look of disappointment. "Did you not listen to the schedule?"

Before the door slammed, Corala added, "Pay attention."

I turned about to face the prison cell.

It was warm in appearance, quite large, and – actually, quite nice. It may have been a prison cell in function; it was anything but that in design.

One large room, about thirty feet by fifty feet. Four thick rugs covered the stone floor. The walls were decorated with several framed portraits. The left side of the room held a Queen-sized, five-post bed. This was an Erskan bed with four posts at the corners and then one attached post at the foot of the bed designed specifically as a whipping post or chain station for the male.

The right side of the room held a chest-high painted-black iron cage which was covered with a thickly-padded black leather cushion. Silver ankle, wrists, and neck chains glinted in the light drawn from a dozen Treaslok candles and four Erskan oil lamps.

One wall held two parallel ten-foot lengths of black-painted wood pegs. An incalculable amount of floggers, cuffs, rope, chain, wood sticks, gloves, and whips were suspended from the pegs.

A shiver ran up my spine.

I inspected the portraits. All of the art had an Erskan female making a heroic pose over a half-cowering naked, collared male. The female in each of the ten portraits wore two or three variations of leather outfits with plenty of chain restraints, whips, or swords. One particular painting displayed a woman that had a striking appearance similar to Tural: facing direct, right hand reaching over her shoulder to draw a sword, cuffs grasped in the left hand. I had a silly grin on my face.

A small table held two flasks of water, a bowl of fruit that appeared Treaslok in origin, and several small glass cylinders. I popped the cork-like top off one cylinder and waved it under my nose.

It had a sweet scent. I poured a bit onto my fingertips.

The liquid was light and slippery.

I tested three other tubes; each had a different consistency and scent, but all appeared to be intended as a lubricant or a massage oil.

The far side of the room was a rectangular pillow "pit." Approximately twenty or more pillows lay scattered about on a cushion floor. Three slave rings hung from the stone wall by the pillow pit.

A glance around the room confirmed that a slave ring was secured to the wall in five foot intervals.

Three rings were suspended from the stone ceiling.

I went to the bed.

As expected, each corner had chains permanently welded to the frame.

Chains, slave rings, torture and bondage furniture. It was a typical Erskan bedroom.

One hour of rest.

I knew that sleep would be difficult.

Except my stomach was full; the lights dim, the room scented, and the temperature slightly cool.

I crawled under the sheets and my naked body warmed. The pillows were of the same construction that Tural favored. My arms wrapped around two pillows and smashed them under my chin.

They reminded me of Tural's pillows.

The scent.

Silky-smooth texture.

The scent.

It was from Tural! She had these placed here!

The silly grin formed on my face again.

The way the pillows found their niche under my shoulders.

And...

"Alexi!"

My eyes opened.

Did I fall asleep?

I rolled over to my left side.

Virsa stood, her curvaceous silhouette filling the doorframe.

"Yes, Mistress!" I jumped to the floor. I ran to her feet and kissed her boots.

My reaction was habitual.

She stepped aside and pointed to the fortified door.

Corala opened it and pointed to the end of the hallway.

I followed Corala to the bathroom.

Instead of being led to a tub they directed me to a shower area.

"Be still," Virsa told me.

Corala pulled a hose from a table and proceeded to spray me with warm water.

Virsa tossed a round-shaped bar to me.

I quickly soaped.

Corala rinsed my body.

Both women produced oversized towels and dried my skin.

They rubbed a light oil on my back and shoulders. Virsa rubbed the same on my inner thighs.

Virsa circled my body twice, inspecting. She cocked her head and looked at Corala. Then she looked at me. "The scars may not be well received. We do not know."

"My scars, Mistress?"

She sighed. "It is not normal to discuss this with a breeding frey."

Corala nodded. "He is not normal."

The main door opened and Deasa, Mistress of the Sa doh-La, entered. She was followed by two females, one dressed as the breeding guards, and another attired in a simple outfit comprised of snug leather pants and leather vest. She was probably an aide in training.

Other than my collar I was completely naked. I kept my wrists behind my back in the standard posture.

Deasa took a position behind me as I looked slightly downward to the floor. She circled around me once.

"It is not only the scars that concerns," Deasa said.

"I believe they will know by tomorrow," Virsa said.

What were they talking about?

Deasa reached over and pressed her right-hand pointer finger onto a scar on my right thigh. She moved her finger down several inches until the scar faded.

"Still...." Deasa said.

I couldn't stand it anymore.

"Mistress?" I asked.

Deasa and Virsa looked at me.

"I do not understand."

Deasa sighed.

"Cultural," Corala said.

"Of course," Deasa replied in an almost irritated tone. "Of course."

Deasa took my chin in her hand and pointed my eyes at hers. "Erskan civilian women are not accustomed to seeing men with battle scars. We are concerned that the civilians will... will not find you attractive."

"Oh," was all I could say.

That was the last thing I thought an Erskan woman would think. It was a warrior culture!

"Erskan women," Deasa continued, "prefer the skin of a man smooth to the touch on the outside, rock-hard on the inside. Other than a brand of ownership, Erskan women do not want to view a permanent scar. Short, insignificant lines on the body are permissible; but heavy marks such as those on your legs and back..."

My legs trembled as the thought occurred to me; my chin slipped out of Deasa's grasp.

Corala reached out to my shoulder and supported my weight for a half-second. I gathered myself and stood.

"That mother fucker," I said in English. "That goddamned mother fucker."

"In Erskan!" Deasa demanded.

I clenched my teeth and looked at each of them. "That is why Corrigan and Ineer whipped frey Mermak and I. To physically demean us."

"From the stories I have heard, that could be the reasoning," Deasa said, her right hand cradling her chin. "The past is what it is. I am concerned with the now and what is to become."

Corala released her grasp. I put my wrists behind my back again.

"Mistress Deasa," the aide said. "Ten minutes."

"The first woman you will service is a former Erskan military officer," Deasa told me. "I expect that she will have more understanding of your physical condition. Like all of the women you will service, fertility is her primary goal. I suffered a debate on whether to discuss this situation with you. I am aware that the male can only sustain a certain level of criticism about his physical attributes without becoming upset or pensive; however, you should be aware of the cultural history and expectations of those which come to be impregnated. Do not take rejection about the appearance of your body in a personal manner."

"What about my missing teeth?" I asked.

All four women laughed.

"No woman will see your face," Deasa said. "Never identify yourself by name. You are merely the property of Deasa, Mistress of the Sa doh-La."

"The women are not here to have a conversation with you," Virsa grinned. "They only want you for rogging."

"Mistress, please pardon the interruption, but I think my identity will be known."

Deasa and Virsa nodded.

"It is only a matter of time," Deasa told me. "The sequence was made several months ago without regard to the male breeder."

"Breeding Room Sixteen," Virsa told the aide.

"All is ready," she replied.

Deasa stretched her arm and took my penis into her hand. "Do not disappoint me. Twenty lashes with a four-foot whip if I receive a report of unsatisfactory sexual performance."

She jerked her hand to accentuate the "performance."

"Yes, Mistress Deasa," I humbly replied.

Virsa moved to the door, opened it, and waited for me to proceed her into the hall.

Corala unlocked my Breeding Room and led me inside while Virsa stood in the doorframe.

"Center of room, kneel."

I faced the door and went to my knees.

"Palms out, face down position," Corala ordered.

I bent over forward and took the prostrated position with my palms flat, thumbs touching. It was the most docile position a slave could take, known as the formal presentation position. The other position was much more informal and was that which Tural preferred me to present: kneeling with knees apart, genitals exposed, wrists crossed high at the back, eyes lowered.

It came to me that the Erskan military was, like Earth's armed forces, less refined in some social areas. The breeding area here appeared to be civilian-oriented, which probably meant a different style of decorum.

Of course, many of my previous estimates of Erskan culture were frequently incorrect. I had much to learn.

"Lift your head," Corala said.

She moved behind me and straddled my waist with her legs. She pulled a leather hood over my head.

Corala tugged on it until it was snug.

The leather scent permeated my nostrils and I closed my eyes and savored the deep breath that naturally came to me.

"How is the position?" she asked.

"Good, Mistress," I replied. A relaxed calm enveloped my naked body.

Corala tightened the laces on the rear of the hood. She tied the laces through a leather strap. Then the leather strap was wrapped around my throat twice.

Four small locks were snapped into place around the strap. It was secured to the outside and slightly below my steel collar, effectively blocking an attempt to read the markings of my ownership.

A single steel circle was positioned in the hood at my lips. The diameter allowed the tip of my tongue to enter, but not push all the way through.

It also served as the solitary breathing hole.

Corala's boots shuffled on the rug until they met the stone floor at the door. They shut and locked the door.

I waited for the woman.

And waited.

My shoulders became sore.

My time as an Erskan slave had taught me a level of patience I did not previously possess. In fact, I often found myself susceptible in relaxing to the point of dozing off.

Which would not be acceptable here.

The hood was dark, which further hampered my effort to stay fully awake.

The door opened and slammed.

Involuntarily my body twitched.

The volume of my breathing was amplified by the tight leather hood.

I could feel a presence in the room.

On my left side.

The tips of her fingers teased the back of my hair at the neck.

"Netra," she said under her breath.

Did she see the scars on my legs? Was she displeased?

"Ah, yes. Yes."

She placed the palm of her right hand fully against my spine and eased her hand down to my buttocks.

Then she slid her left hand along my spine. It was a soothing motion.

My shoulders tingled.

"I have seen you from a distance," she said. Her voice was scratchy, almost hoarse. "The personal property of the Secera Torino. This is –"

She moved behind me and pressed her body against mine. A leather bra caressed my shoulder blades. Warm skin at her midriff drew my back slightly toward her.

"This is a pleasant surprise," she finished speaking.

The tone of her voice was neutral. I could not ascertain if she was genuinely pleased in a favorable manner or – one in which she wanted to extract revenge. It was a matter of perspective.

"Lie flat!" she ordered.

I pulled my legs to the side in preparation of laying flat; however her hand shoved the small of my back and pushed me to the rug.

My air went out with a "woof" sound when my stomach flattened.

Her fingers wrapped around the back of my neck and took in a handful of slack leather.

"Hands outstretched to the sides."

I complied.

She walked to my right side.

My fingertips cringed as she brought her shoe or boot onto them – easy at first and then with a painful portion of her body weight.

I groaned, but did not try to pull my hand away.

She released the pressure but moved her heel along the lower part of my arm, along the triceps muscle, and then to my right side at the ribs.

"On all fours," she said.

I got to my hands and knees.

She clutched onto the back of my collar and dragged me. My legs and hands struggled to keep pace with her.

She lifted on the collar and I felt the metal bed frame with my hands. I climbed onto the bed.

She jerked the collar farther to the bed and I crawled to about the middle.

Chains rattled and in a moment she locked one at the back of the leather hood.

"Flat," she ordered.

I lay on my stomach again.

She yanked my wrists back and secured both with closely-connected metal manacles. Locks clicked as they secured her victim.

A tingle ran up my spine.

Instead of having the trepidation that danced with my thoughts the last couple of days I found myself wanting her attention.

With a powerful shove she heaved on my shoulder and rolled me over.

My chest and body was exposed; my wrists behind my buttocks in a slightly painful position. The square corners of the padlocks pressed into my skin. My shoulders strained with the weight of my body against them.

A fingernail pressed against my sternum. She ran it down the center of my chest until reaching my navel.

She laughed when I involuntarily arched my back to press harder into her fingertip.

"You want this, yes?"

I nodded.

"Of course you do. Earthican males are no different than our own in this way."

Her hands pressed onto my chest and then she squeezed my nipples.

"Yes, you react perfectly," she told me. She reached a hand around my thick cock.

"Spread your legs."

I did as told. My back arched again to thrust my pelvis upward.

A metal ankle cuff was locked onto each leg. She threaded chain and then pulled hard.

I groaned as she stretched my body taut. She pulled on my hips until the chain at my neck was equally taut.

It was almost too tight.

Her hands wrapped high around my throat and she squeezed. "You are not permitted to talk; but you will make the sounds I love to hear."

I was unable to nod.

"You are large," she said.

The cushions flexed when she exited the bed.

It was only for a moment. She returned and straddled my thighs.

A cool liquid was poured on my belly. Then both of her hands rubbed it.

I recognized the scent as coming from one of the glass tubes.

My hips rose when both of her wet, slick hands wrapped around my hard erection.

In deliberate, slowly-timed strokes she masturbated my cock for about thirty seconds.

I shifted my wrists slightly and tried to keep the neck chain from choking me.

My legs contracted and pulled on the metal ankle cuffs.

Without a warning, she positioned herself over me and guided my lubricated erection into her.

I moaned as my cock felt her tighten.

Her knees squeezed my thighs and she made two easy strokes on me. Then she slammed down and rammed my cock into her.

My fingers twitched.

Her weight smashed my buttocks into the padlocks.

She slammed me again.

I swallowed as the chain and collar tugged at my neck.

Using my wrists I tried to move upward toward my head, but the metal of the ankle cuffs dug deep into the bone.

She slammed me again.

And again.

I struggled with the painful wrist and ankle cuffs. I groaned in pain when I could, or made muffled sounds when the air was getting cut off.

Yet she did not stop.

She continued to body slam me.

Her hands reached around my thighs and her hands and fingernails squeezed every time she forced my cock to please her.

Her breathing was rapid and deep. Her hips gyrated. One hand let go of my thigh; then I could feel her knuckles under her body, probably masturbating her clitoris as she rogged me.

"You will ejaculate," she said in huffed breaths.

I was barely able to hold it.

My ankles killed me. My wrists and buttocks screamed in pain. And I was not sure that I was still breathing properly.

She slammed again and I instantly exploded.

"Ah!" I moaned.

"Give it all to me," she demanded.

I bucked several times, each more painful on my ankles and neck than the previous reaction.

She pressed a hand on my chest to hold me still.

Then she gyrated for a minute or two and hummed a melody unknown to me.

Without warning, again, she dismounted.

I heard her pulling on clothes.

I could hear laces drawn on boots.

Then the door opened and shut.

I sat motionless for a moment.

Was it a trick? Was she actually standing next to me?

No, I heard her boots on the stone floor by the doorway.

But the leather hood – it cut off the sound.

I waited.

After another long minute or two I relaxed my arms and tried to inch-worm myself closer to the neck chain.

I put in a bit of slack and was able to breathe fully again. The hood was still snug around my neck, but there was nothing pulling.

Except for the ankle cuffs.

And my wrists.

I tried to roll to my right side.

That only increased the stress on my neck and wrists.

I tried to position my wrists to the side.

That was only moderately successful.

No words? She just fucked me and walked out?

Not a "Good slave" or "Next time?"

She just fucked me and left.

I felt "used" in a different way. The Erskan guards and warriors would use me at parties, celebrations, dinner. Okay, well, just about everywhere they wanted to.

But I knew many of them and would see them again. They would say *something* to me after they had used me.

"Excellent oral service, frey!" they would tell me.

Nothing.

What did I expect? Here, I was just a breeder. A sperm machine.

This woman said nothing.

I pulled on the chains and waited.

I wanted out.

I wanted to go back home to the palace.

* * * * *

The door opened with a loud click.

Heels moved across the rug.

I lost track of time, but it seemed like I had been left alone for about an hour.

My fingertips were numb.

My toes were cold.

And it was the longest after sex that I had been left with bodily fluids over my body.

The neck chain was unlocked.

I allowed a soft moan of relief.

"Poor frey," Virsa consoled.

"Good report on you," Corala added.

The cuffs on my ankles snapped open.

"Oh," I huffed. I pulled my feet together and rubbed the right inner ankle with the toes on my left foot.

"Stand, on your right," Virsa ordered.

I groaned and tossed my feet over the side of the bed. Then with a minor hesitation I got to my feet.

The wrist cuffs were unlocked.

I pulled my hands to the side and then crossed them in front of my body to rub the wrists.

Even though I had not been struck by anything, I felt as though my entire body had been thoroughly beaten.

They unlocked the damp, leather hood and pulled it from my head. A couple of the room's candles were nearly burned to the bottom. I must have been in here for two or more hours.

Virsa snapped a chain-link leash to my collar and walked out of the room.

I followed her to the bathing room.

They put me in the tub and repeated the cleaning routine, complete with hands held outstretched for an eternity.

I was given cold water to drink and then taken back into Breeding Room Sixteen. Someone replaced the bedding while I was gone.

A replacement hood was pulled over my head and I was told to assume the waiting position in the center of the room.

There I waited for about two hours, oftentimes shuffling my feet or changing the position of my knees.

My emotions were numb. I didn't feel like thinking of anything or anyone.

I wanted to go home to the palace.

But I could be here for years.

This would be my daily routine?

Sex, bathing, eat, sex, bathing, sex?

Admittedly, I was more than a little intrigued about the role of being a breeder. Sex with as many women as I could have. Wow.

So far...

This was only one instance. My first.

But... What would be different with the second woman? She would be visiting me for one thing: to get pregnant. Not for conversation. Not for companionship.

Just sex.

I wasn't sure that I could get it up so quick, anyhow. Perhaps three or four hours already.

That had not been a problem before. I was just making up problems so –

The door unlocked.

I steadied my kneeling position and kept my breathing light.

She wasted no time in approaching me.

Two hands reached between my legs and grabbed my scrotum and penis.

She squeezed. Tighter.

I groaned.

She squeezed tighter.

My eyes watered and my breaths came out in hard, choppy sounds.

"Urg!" I exclaimed.

She released her grasp.

Rope encircled my right ankle, then my left. They were about shoulder-width apart and could move no farther.

She bound my wrists behind me with rope, close to one another.

My wrists were jerked back and then tied to my ankles.

Another rope, smaller in size I believed, was wrapped around my cock and balls. She tightened it and then connected it to the rope between my ankles.

The constriction around my cock made the blood stay in; I was unable to prevent the erection that appeared within moments.

She tied another rope to the cock and ball bondage. This was tugged slightly forward.

Her positioning of my knees and feet allowed moderate stability.

I could sense her body directly in front of me.

A lubricated hand clutched at my erection.

She held my cock still as she guided herself back onto it.

I finally realized she was mounting me from a doggy-style position.

She rubbed my cock against her. I moaned as the sensitive tip of my cock strained to push past her lips and fully enter her.

With a shove of her hand, she backed her body fully into mine and thrust my hard erection inside.

My cock and balls were pulled forward. She used the rope with her hands to control my cock.

Her rhythm was fast and furious.

The cock and ball rope forced me into her. She pulled harder and harder on the lines.

My cock was sore.

My balls hung low and painfully swung with each thrust.

"Frey, do not wait to ejaculate!" she demanded.

Tural and the warriors had so often instructed me to not have an orgasm until they had theirs – or for several days at a time. I had been trained to *not* cum immediately.

"Now!" she screamed.

The tension of the rope around my cock was almost too much.

"Now, frey!" she screamed.

The inevitable and unstoppable orgasm lit my mind and body. It rocked my body and I came.

She jerked on the rope and held my cock in her as I bucked into her.

I pressed against her body and tried to soak in her warmth.

She pulled away.

I moaned.

She made a curt laugh.

The rope around my cock and balls was loosened and then removed.

I remained on my knees, panting.

She reached over my back, took the ropes from my wrists to ankles in-hand, and then shoved me down to my left side.

I fell onto the rug with a slight thud onto my left shoulder.

She wiped her hands on my right buttock and flank.

The door opened and was shut.

My right flank was covered in body fluids again.

No. This wasn't to my liking.

At least I was not forced to stay on my knees.

After a few minutes of lying still, my breathing returned to normal and I fell asleep.

* * * * *

After a silent bath, I ate lunch alone in Meal Room Sixteen.

It was a good meal consisting predominantly of Erskan fare and a few unknown items that I assumed were Treaslok.

Virsa and Corala did not have much to say.

And I felt like any questions or conversation would be useless.

Tural said she would come for me in four days. Was that three days now? Or four days?

I picked at the warm red beans on my clay plate.

The heavy security made sense. I understood why a man would try to escape this place.

I pushed the plate to the side of the table after eating only half of the food. I did drink my fill of water.

The door was unlocked.

Virsa latched the chain leash around my collar.

I was led to Breeding Room Sixteen, hooded, and positioned.

The third woman appeared within a few minutes. She dragged me to the bed, tied my arms and ankles wide apart, and fucked me for a half-hour before telling me to orgasm. She wiped my body with a towel, kissed the hood at my forehead, and then walked out singing.

It appeared that each session would last three hours, whether the woman used it or not.

The restraints were less tight than the previous instances; she was probably a civilian.

Virsa and Corala retrieved me, gave me a bath, and had me rest in Sleeping Quarters Sixteen for an hour.

Then they dragged me back to Breeding Room Sixteen and put me in service again.

Several hours later, both guards put me in Sleeping Quarters Sixteen for the night.

I had serviced six women during the day. Two in the morning, two after lunch, and two in the evening.

I feel asleep the instant my head landed on the pillow. It was a pillow I'm certain Tural had delivered for me.

* * * * *

The next day was almost more of the same. Though one woman bailed. She came into the room, waited a minute, and left.

I serviced five women during the second day.

Again sleep was welcome and immediate.

* * * * *

Virsa finished setting the fourth lock about the hood.

"You are quiet, frey," Corala said.

"Yes, Mistress."

"You are not happy," Corala said. Was it a question or a statement.

Tural told me to tell the truth. I admitted to them, "I do not want to be here."

"That is typical," Virsa said.

A hand was put on my shoulder.

Virsa continued, "You may not view the women. They have no interest in you personally. This is the way that it is."

I did not want to do this for months or years. I couldn't!

Tears rolled out of my eyes and were absorbed by the lining of the leather hood.

"He is crying," Corala said.

"No, I am not," I lied.

To do this every day...

"Cancel this morning," Virsa said. She loosened the hood and pulled it from my head.

Unexpectedly, she took my face and pressed it to her breast.

"You must do your duty, yes?"

"Yes, Mistress."

Tears rolled off my face.

"I will allow you a rest this morning, frey. After the mid-day meal you will be rid of your selfishness and be prepared to perform as your owner expects. Yes?"

"Thank you, Mistress," I told her.

"Lay down here," Virsa said. She guided my head to the rug.

They walked out and locked the door behind them.

For a moment I sobbed.

Then I shook my head.

Why was I crying?

Fuck!

How could a man get emotional over this?

I wiped my eyes dry and sat cross-legged.

I would not dishonor Tural by failing to perform willingly.

Unconditional surrender. That is what I have to give.

Unconditional.

I was her frey and I would act like one.

My hands wiped my face again.

I looked at the door.

Should I go to the door and get their attention?

I was ready.

Unconditional surrender. I will meet my obligations.

It was only a few days until the Glow Ceremony.

Or two days.

Three?

The door flung open.

Deasa burst inside and nearly ran to my position.

I cringed.

Was she displeased that Virsa had allowed me rest as a result of my personal pity party?

She reached a hand out to mine.

"There is a problem," she told me. "Get up!"

I took her hand.

She pulled me to my feet.

Virsa and Corala came rushing from the door at the other end of the hall – the door I never went through.

"Find his palace skirt," Deasa told Corala. "Front room, immediately."

"Understood," Corala replied. She ran ahead to the door before us.

"What has happened?" Virsa asked.

I followed Deasa through the door and into the bathing area.

Two other guards bathed a male while he sat in the center tub. All three of them turned to look at us with a surprised expression.

We went past them to another set of doors. It was Deasa's office.

"Korina Jurina Cinzia issued an urgent dispatch. Alexi is required in the Council immediately. I do not know why. Two Elite Guards will be here in a moment." Deasa went to the single window and looked outside. "There is much activity in the courtyard. Two or three harfala have appeared within the last ten minutes."

Virsa looked beside Deasa. "Yes. Maybe we can find –"

The door to Deasa's office opened.

Cinzia was dressed in combat uniform and was flanked by two Elite Guards, Simona, an Erskan, and Igo, a Treaslok.

"A thousand pardons, Lady Deasa," Cinzia said. "This is of the utmost importance. The Torino sends her profound regret at the interruption."

"Jurina Cinzia," Deasa replied, moving toward her. "You of all women know that I understand the matters of state!"

Cinzia and Deasa hugged.

"Are you permitted to tell me what has happened?" Deasa asked.

Cinzia released her grasp and stood back. She looked at me. "Alexi, are you well?"

"Yes, Mistress Cinzia, I am. Deasa and her staff are most efficient and professional."

"Good." Cinzia looked at Deasa, Virsa, and at Corala, whom had arrived with my belongings in a rectangular wicker basket. "Alexi, we have just received a messenger from the Busai. She is speaking with the Torino at this moment."

"What does she want?" I asked. My hands expertly buckled my full-length, black leather open-side skirt about my waist.

"To talk to you."

I paused and allowed my left boot to remain unlaced. "To me?"

"She has something to show to you. We do not know what it is."

I finished both boots and handed the basket to Corala with a "Thank you."

Then I approached Deasa, kissed her boots, and sought to do the same for Virsa.

Cinzia tugged on my skirt, "Sorry, no time for formalities."

I nodded to Virsa and Corala and followed Cinzia and her escort.

We made a full-speed run down six flights of stairs until entering the Council of Jurinas.

Every staffed position in Tural's Council had a representative sitting and listening intently to Tural.

Tural was at the head of the room. She stood with her hands on hip, fingers tapping. I recognized her expression: she was angry but was intent on projecting a face of impatience.

Four Elite Guards encircled a seated woman, also on the dais with Tural.

Cinzia grabbed my hand and pulled me to the front of the room.

On habit, I headed for Tural's boots. She stayed my position by raising her palm toward me.

"Alexi, this is Ro. She is a Busai officer sent by Kale. You remember my account of Kale?"

Kale was the leader of the Busai that had set a trap for Tural. Tural wounded Kale and killed Kale's sister in the ensuing battle.

Ro appeared calm and relaxed, as though she held the winning cards to a poker game. Her hair was short and black. Multiple silver rings pierced her ears. She had a stud that pierced her lower lip.

She wore a brown leather halter top, sleeveless, that was buckled in the front by a strap at a forty-five degree angle. She wore tight brown leather pants, dark brown knee-high, lace-front boots, and a wide black belt. Her arms were crossed and hands rested in her lap. Muscles in her thighs were accentuated by the shine of leather in the well-lit room. In Earth society I would have identified Ro as a butch lesbian.

Ro reciprocated the visual examination.

I may be an Erskan slave, but I was Erskan foremost. I was not the slightest bit submissive to any woman that was the enemy of my people.

Especially when it came to anyone that had tried to kill Tural.

I faced Ro and crossed my arms before me. The muscles in my biceps rippled and I used my height to peer down at the enemy.

Ro laughed. "This is the Earth male."

Her Treaslok was fairly well-pronounced.

"I am Alexi, frey of Tural," I told her.

"So you are. So you are."

"He is here now, Ro," Tural said in Treaslok. Tural pointed to an Elite Guard.

The guard approached with a black steel case of Earth origin.

"They do not know what this is," Ro said, followed by a laugh. "But you will."

The guard released the case latch and opened the lid.

Though the padded case was empty, my heart skipped a beat.

A bold yellow and black sticker clearly indicated the nuclear nature of the missing device.

"Fuck!" I said in English.

Tural moved over to look. "What is it?"

Ro laughed again.

I looked at the label.

"CTSL-XT5 Authorized Use Only – Warning – Thermonuclear Ordinance."

I faced Ro and resisted reaching down and tearing her body apart.

"A bomb," I told her. "A very powerful bomb."

"You know that Kale struck a bargain with Lewis Corrigan," Ro told me. She stood and walked to me. Ro took the box in her hand and sat again. The box rest on her lap and she tapped her fingers across the metal surface.

"Yes. You capture the Treaslok people and Corrigan would have given me over to you," I said.

Several of the Treaslok officers appeared surprised.

Ro laughed again. I observed that her laugh equally irritated all in the

Council.

"Yes, we capture Dola, give it back to Ineer and Corrigan, and we keep you. Kale does not want Treaslok prisoners. She only wants you. Now you have no choice."

Ro stood to her feet and cocked her head. "I will take him with me, now, or Dola will be destroyed."

There was a momentary pause and then a ripple of laughter about the room.

Tural and Cinzia did not laugh. Both looked at me.

"Where is the bomb?" I demanded.

"It may be in this room," Ro grinned. "Or in a market."

She withdrew a small red metal pin from her purse and handed it to me.

"Detonator – Remove Pin to Activate" was written on a red plastic card.

She took the pin from my hand. "I have been told that the range of this hand-machine can be several hundred tachets. More than enough distance to stand by and watch."

I relaxed my hands and let them drop to the side. "Yes. I will go with you."

Jurina Monu broke the silence, "What?"

Tural jumped to her feet. She had no sword, but her hand went to her right boot, ready to draw a Stac-Gun.

I raised my palm to Tural and held it there for a few seconds. "Tell Netratoh Peto that I will be leaving through the gate with Ro. I do not see any other option."

"Alexi," Tural asked. "I will not be coerced by this threat!"

"It was placed in the city before Corrigan left," Ro added.

"How will I know that you have not detonated the bomb?" I asked. "I demand monthly visitations at the gate."

"Three months," Ro said.

"Alexi!" Tural demanded. "What are you doing?"

Though it caused mental anguish, I turned away from my Mistress and faced Ro. "What do you want with me?"

"You will talk to our engineers."

"For how long?"

"Until we desire."

Tural grabbed my shoulder. "Alexi!"

"This is a storage case for a bomb," I switched to Erskan and pointed to the box in Ro's hands. "The control machine is not here. The control machine can allow a person thousands of miles away to make a great explosion. The bomb that Ro says is here in Dola will destroy everything."

There was a murmur of surprise among the Erskans and Erskan-speaking Treaslok officers.

Tural put her left hand around my right bicep. Her touch was soft but her eyes burned. "Destroy everything? How is that possible?"

"It is a nuclear weapon. It would completely obliterate everything here. No buildings would remain, no bodies, no trees, nothing. It would look worse than the Yiminee Desert. Three million people killed in less than ten seconds."

Cinzia's face turned white.

"Ten seconds?" Tural repeated.

"Less, actually."

"We can use yours on them first," Cinzia said.

"I don't have one of those," I replied.

"We will search for it and remove it," Monu offered.

"It is about the size of a person's head," I told them, indicating the empty box. "It could be anywhere. None of the Earth machines I have here can find the bomb."

"Are you done begging?" Ro asked, in Treaslok. "We go now."

"I am not giving you away," Tural said. Her grip tightened on my arm.

"Do you see any option?" I asked.

"Is it a trick?" Cinzia asked.

"The storage case is authentic. There is no way of knowing if the bomb is really here or not." I shook my head.

"When we find this machine..." Tural said.

"Take the bomb to the mountains and bury it," I told them. "Then get away. The explosion will destroy everything in a thirty-five mile radius. Everything."

"Why do you have such weapons?" Monu asked.

"We will find it," Tural said to me. Then she faced Ro and spoke in Treaslok: "Someday, Ro, I will have your head for this outrage."

"One press of a metal button and the west coast is gone forever. I do not care what you want." Ro walked to the door and then stopped to look over her shoulder.

The Elite Guards were powerless to do anything. Their hands flexed around cold swords.

I knelt down and kissed Tural's boots.

She pulled me to her mouth and kissed me.

"Survive, Alexi," she said in English. "I will come for you. Do what you need to survive."

"I know you will," I said.

"Slave!" Ro ordered in the Treaslok language.

I kissed Tural again and then turned about.

Before walking out I stole a glance over my shoulder: Tural slowly collapsed onto her throne. Monu reached to console her. Cinzia moved toward other officers to engage in a heated discussion. Visada quietly slipped out of the room.

Several Erskan and Treaslok guards flanked us on our walk to four Busai-equipped horses. Apparently Ro and I were in store for a long ride.

I expected my wrists to be bound to the saddle. So invincible did the Busai feel that she did not bother to place me in bondage.

I sat high in the saddle.

I would allow no one would see my true feelings of helplessness.

Despair would not rule my thoughts.

There would be a way out of this.

A heavily-armed escort of ten Erskan warriors guided us out of the city and east to the border wall.

Tomorrow was supposed to have been Tural's Glow Ceremony.

Chapter Nineteen
Kale's Gift

The four-hour ride to the gate was solemn. None of the Erskan officers said anything. They had only time to receive short instructions from Cinzia and probably did not know the background of what was happening.

I was certain that Netratoh Peto, in charge of the center gate, was already informed via radio of the situation.

Peto and two other officers, all mounted on horseback, blocked the road to the closed and barred gate. Hundreds of Erskan and Treaslok warriors stood in formation near the gate, ready to take arms if required. Another two-thousand warriors were out of view – so that the Busai did not have accurate intelligence on our defenses.

"Stop," Peto ordered, raising a hand.

"As I told you this morning, my business is with the Torino, not with you," Ro sneered.

"That is no longer the case," Peto told her. "I will talk with the Torino's property alone."

Ro looked at the sky. The sun was on its cescent to the west. It was probably about six in the afternoon. "You answer your Erskan Mistress well."

Peto merely grinned. She looked at her thumb and then placed it on the top of the hilt of the sword at her hip. "The Erskans helped rid us of Eji Ineer and *her* Master, the Earth male Corrigan. You should be grateful to Torino Tural. It was not our regular warrior force that burned your villages. But now you threaten all of my people and take Tural's property."

I noticed that Peto was careful not to reveal that she miraculously possessed information from Dola's Council Chambers.

Ro leaned slightly over the side of her horse and spat on the dirt road. She looked toward the gate and wiped her lips. "The eight Swod will be appeased."

Peto wrapped her fingers around her sword. She eased it up an inch and exposed steel.

Ro laughed: "You want the blood of millions on your sword?"

Peto's eyebrows narrowed and she leaned forward. "I will talk with the frey. Now."

Ro shrugged and gave in: "The richta need water. You may have a moment with him." Ro moved her horse slightly to the right of Peto.

Peto released her hand and guided her horse a few feet off the path to make way.

"Off," Ro told me.

I dismounted and handed the reins to Ro. She took all three horses to a watering trough about sixty feet ahead.

Peto and the other two officers dismounted.

"I received the radio call four hours ago from Jurina Cinzia. Is there nothing we can do to find this exploding bomb?"

I shook my head, "The science is so far ahead."

I looked over my shoulder toward the west. "Peto, if there really is a bomb in Dola, you would feel it here, two hundred miles away. We cannot take the chance. It would kill everyone in the city."

"Then...what, Alexi?"

"I do not know. The Tamagra space wagon is unlocked now; Uimisla could try to fix the radiation detector. Oh, she doesn't even know what 'radiation' means or how to re-wire anything in there. It's..." I trailed off. Even I had slim odds of jury-rigging something from the left-over debris of the ship. Nuclear devices were not my core field. This was only the second time I had even come close to a real nuclear-related device. Ro only had the storage case and a detonator pin.

It was not too difficult to believe Ro's story. Sheri took away six canisters of highly-illegal nerve gas. Corrigan could have had a nuclear bomb as an insurance policy.

I should have turned him over to Tural for interrogation.

Then execution.

Peto reached out and held onto my biceps. Her face was serious. "Alexi, the Busai are not like us. They are always traveling. Their cities hardly deserve the word. They are small places for trading. Most of the Busai live on the grass beyond the gate. It is a hard life."

Peto looked over her shoulder and increased the speed of her talking, "It is a hard life. There are eight Swod. Kale is the leader of all. But only for two years. The leadership rotates among the eight. I do not know where they are in the cycle but –"

"Slave!"

I turned over my shoulder. Ro mounted her horse and pointed at mine. She grabbed the reins of the other two spare horses.

I knew better than to waste precious time interrupting Peto.

Peto released my left arm and she slowly guided us toward Ro. "Tural cannot see you in three months' time. The Busai cannot suspect that you are fertile. Be very careful about challenging any males. You are a big male and a good fighter, but their males work in tight packs –"

"Slave!" Ro demanded again.

Peto held my arm and we stopped out of earshot of Ro. Peto looked in my eyes, "Watch the Orphans. They will help you navigate. And watch for the storms. They are both dangerous – and a means of freedom when the time is right."

Ro brought the horses to us.

Peto took the reins and handed them to me.

I pulled myself onto the horse and looked down at the three Treaslok officers.

There was no other option.

I chose to remain on Aervanta because it was a life I never knew existed, and it was now a life that I could not lose.

I had confirmed my slave heart by serving Tural and the Erskans by being a breeder.

My Mistress carried our baby.

I will survive.

"Shia-Talso," Peto said as she snapped an Erskan salute.

A breeze rippled my palace skirt. I put my boots into the stirrups. Then I returned the salute, straightened my body, and followed Ro to the open gate.

A hundred brave warriors, Erskan and Treaslok, watched our approach from the top walkway along the wall and over the gate. They were silent and unmoving.

Lining the wall were colorful Erskan flags and banners, flapping in the wind.

We crossed under the gate and faced the flat, open expanse.

Several dozen mounted Busai warriors waited a few hundred feet distant on the flat grassy plains. They had their own flags and were clustered around one group of riders. Kale was probably there, waiting for a frightened and intimidated prisoner.

The massive gate closed with a secure and solid impact behind me, but I refused to turn around to see.

I squared my shoulders, tightened my grip on the reins, and caught Ro by surprise as I galloped past her toward the center of the enemy line.

Fem Fist Books

About the Author

K. McVey has been a rubber fetish st and BDSM enthusiast since the 1980s.

His novels blend life-long passions for science fiction and adventure with pulse pounding erotic dominance & submission.

When not traveling to kink events throughout the world, he collects original fetish art to complement a growing latex and leatherwear wardrobe. K. lives in the USA with pet racing motorcycles.